BONACHON BLOOD

Bonachon is a law-abiding town on the western edge of the Mojave Desert. But waiting on the outskirts is someone who wants to change all that. Colvin Datch carries a grudge from a crooked past, and when Sheriff Jeff Kayte is killed, the townsfolk are shaken. Ruben Ballard can't stand by and watch a small group of desperate men take over. When a few loyal townsfolk offer their support, he decides to pick up a Colt — but Datch and his allies are ready to fight . . .

CALEB RAND

BONACHON
BLOOD

Complete and Unabridged

LINFORD
Leicester

First published in Great Britain in 2016 by
Robert Hale
an imprint of The Crowood Press
Wiltshire

First Linford Edition
published 2019
by arrangement with
The Crowood Press
Wiltshire

A catalogue record for this book is available
from the British Library.

ISBN 978–1–4448–4077–3

Published by
F. A. Thorpe (Publishing)
Anstey, Leicestershire

Set by Words & Graphics Ltd.
Anstey, Leicestershire
Printed and bound in Great Britain by
T. J. International Ltd., Padstow, Cornwall

This book is printed on acid-free paper

1

'That's Jefferson Kayte, sheriff of Bonachon. Take a good look, son . . . see the way of him. It's somethin' you'll have to learn, 'cause damn soon it'll be *you* out there impressin' these good folk.'

Colvin Datch eased the old supply wagon against the boardwalk. He sat back in the seat, let his stare travel the full length of the narrow street ahead. Rancor showed in his eyes, seemed to snick a corner of his mouth as he spoke to the youngster beside him.

'When we get down let *me* do the talkin',' he continued. 'Don't say nothin' unless I look to you. Not a word. We don't want to go foulin' things up. You hear me, son?'

Bruno Datch had seen the sheriff walking towards them. He nodded, gritted his teeth as if it helped his concentration. 'Yeah, I hear you, Pa. I'll do like you say,' he agreed.

Colvin Datch climbed from the wagon, slapped a hand against his coat to shake out the range dust. It was his best, store-bought outfit, similar in everything but size to the one he'd insisted Bruno wore. He cast a swift look in the direction of the approaching lawman, hesitating a moment before stepping up from the street.

Inside the office of the town jail, he motioned for Bruno to remove his flop-brimmed hat, stand to one side of the front door.

'Remember, not a word,' he repeated. 'If you let me handle it, come sundown, you'll be wearin' one o' them shiny stars, like I promised.'

Bruno appeared to be on the verge of asking a question, but his father's glowering look silenced him.

Moments later, footsteps sounded on the boards and a big man's frame filled the doorway of the office. It was late afternoon, and the western sun cast

Jefferson Kayte's shadow halfway across the room. The man's face appeared calm, carried no feature which a stranger might be taken with; nothing to recall later, unless it was the inscrutable, pale grey eyes.

But Kayte's expression had tightened the moment he'd seen Colvin Datch and his son haul up in front of his office.

'What can I do for you, Datch?' he asked brusquely.

Datch forced a tolerant look. 'We've come for a talk. Me an' Bruno's got an offer to make.'

Kayte turned to the youth. 'You don't want to get behind me, boy. Stand where I can see you,' he said, waving him further into the room. 'You haven't got trust on your side.'

With his gaze fixed on Bruno, Kayte walked to his desk, pulled out a chair and slumped down. It had been a long, hot day and most of the troubles he'd encountered had only been brought on by the oppressive heat. He was tired and wanted a drink, was in no mood for anyone to make him offers he had to think too much about.

'Bruno's reached a size and an' age when he needs work,' Datch started. 'He's a good boy, listens up an' does what he's told. I figured you could take him in an' show him the ropes. Maybe . . . '

Kayte's jaw dropped. 'That's the offer? Your boy in my office?' he rasped. 'Hell, Datch, any kin o' yours is lucky if they haven't already been shown a hangman's *rope*.'

'That ain't funny, Kayte. The boy's learned real good. *You* just show an' tell. Give *him* a chance to prove himself.'

Kayte's look was shifting from irritation to growing amusement. He half grinned, shook his head at realizing Datch was serious. 'I'll give you an' him the chance to clear off. That's what I'll give.'

Colvin Datch didn't move. It looked like he'd predicted Kayte's response, and it hadn't touched him badly.

'You got no right to hold against my boy what you hold against me, Sheriff. No right. Abe Lincoln wouldn't have taken kindly to them thoughts.'

'He'd never have known what I do, Datch. Now get yourselves from my office.'

'I'm not wantin' somethin' for *me*, goddamn it. I wouldn't expect it. But Bruno ain't done wrong. He knows his signs an' ciphers ... never been involved with wrong 'uns. What's to go against him?'

'Family association. I don't know much else about him, and that's the way I'd like it to stay. I wouldn't sleep well at night listenin' for a Datch footfall.' To show the encounter was over, Kayte raised himself from the desk.

Datch's expression hardened, and when Bruno looked his way, he grunted, 'Leave us. Wait outside. Me an' the sheriff needs to rope in some personal stuff.'

Bruno picked up his hat that Kayte was already pushing across the desk towards him. He shrugged casually and went out to the boardwalk. Datch closed the door after him, his manner changing as he turned.

'Goddamn you, Kayte,' he grated. 'Some other time, some other place, I'd smack you one for talkin' to me like that . . . in front of the boy, an' all. I've spent years schoolin' young Bruno in how to mix with people . . . how to be good — observant of the law.'

Kayte held up his hand. 'Can it. You're not harmless, stranger. Some other time, in some other place, I was tryin' my damndest to get you put away for murder as well as robbery. You were cleared by a court, but not me. Never by me. You're vermin, an' I don't ever want you or any o' your kin in my town. As for holdin' any sort of office, it'll be over my dead body.'

Datch clasped his hands firmly on the edge of the desk. He bit his lip on the obvious reply, continuing the push for his son. 'Bruno's done schoolin',' he persisted.

'I've no doubt. But in what?' Kayte said. 'I'm only listenin' now because he needs some sort o' payback for havin' *you* as a father. No, you're up to somethin', Datch, an' this is your first move. I can smell it on you.'

A nerve under Colvin Datch's right eye twitched. 'You ain't much of a lawman, Kayte. Holding something against a man all these years. You think bein' distrustful's a finer quality . . . somethin' better?'

'It's a safety measure. I remember fifteen years back, the look on your face when I turned you in. It was like an open wound that you had to live with because you knew you weren't ever goin' to stand against me. You weren't good enough then, an' you're not now . . . not on your own. That's what I'm lookin' out for.'

'If you're right, Kayte, let's hope you're prepared when the time comes,' Datch snarled.

'I will be. Now, why don't you do somethin' useful for your boy? Take him where your talents are appreciated. I hear Australia's popular right now.'

Datch's chest heaved with emotion. He stepped back and the colour drained from his face, his fingers flexing above the butt of a high-holstered Colt.

Kayte nodded. 'If you want that kid of yours to bury you, go ahead,' he warned, moving resolutely forward. 'Talkin's done.'

Datch muttered threatening curses as he backed off, half turned out through the doorway. Kayte was about to slam the door shut when he caught sight of someone waving, running towards him along the boards.

Milo Prentiss ran right up to the office and drew a couple of eager breaths.

'Best come right away. Stranger at the saloon's callin' for you,' he spluttered.

'Callin' *me*?' Kayte said. 'How'd you mean?'

'It's somethin' to do with the Jewsons,' Prentiss went on, his eyes bulging excitedly. 'I think that's what he said. I was close up to the door an' he pointed at me, said I was to come an' get you . . . Sheriff Kayte. I wasn't goin' to argue. He looks a real ornery critter.'

'Hmm, he'd have to be to get *you* so agitated, Milo,' Kayte replied quietly, like thinking out loud. 'Did he come with a name, you recall?'

'Noble, someone said. Just Noble.' Milo Prentiss, who sorted and stacked at the mercantile, took a step back. It was as though saying a whole name would compromise him even more. 'You know him, Mr Kayte?' he asked.

'Some.' Unmistakable concern crossed Kayte's face. He took a quick look at the gun locker, then at Colvin Datch, before heading off along the boardwalk towards Shelter Saloon.

'When you say thin, you mean real skinny . . . face an' all?' Colvin Datch asked of Prentiss as he stepped down to the street.

9

'Yep, like a piece o' jerky. But he was wearin' duds like one o' them city undertakers.'

Datch nodded. 'If he's who I think he is, that's his business . . . sort of. He ain't called Rites Noble for nothin'.' The man turned to his son, and his eyes flicked around with new enthusiasm. 'Best we go take a look, Bruno. Same as before, just watch unless I say different.' He nudged his son towards their wagon as Prentiss followed on after Kayte. 'Perfect,' he said, taking up the reins. 'If there's a gun-fight, you'll see how they go about their work. Sometimes, chances are where you find 'em.'

Bruno looked puzzled and his father offered no further explanation. He sat stiff and uncertain, looked towards the saloon where a small crowd had already started to gather.

2

Ruben Ballard was in the food store of his stockyard when he heard the fuss. He peered through the fine dust of the window, saw Deputy Silas Layborne unbuckling his gun belt. One of his wranglers was standing back, his fists held up, his chin thrust out defiantly.

Tom Yurling, the yard's stockman, spoke out as soon as he came through the back door of the office. 'Trouble out there, Rube.'

'Yeah, I'm hearing it,' Ballard replied. 'What's it about?'

'A woman. Owen's been goadin' Layborne for a couple of days. Looks like they're takin' it to the next stage.'

Ballard dropped some papers and swore under his breath. He went outside, stood on the step a moment and looked around. Two of the yard workers were moving in with the expectation of trouble. He knew them well enough. Him and Yurling had hand-picked them as honest and hardworking. But right now, he could see them hankering for the fight.

He told them to get back to work as he walked over to one of the cleared pens. Owen Copper was bobbing from foot to foot. He had already removed his shirt, determination spreading across his youthful features.

'It's not your business, boss,' he said. 'It's between me an' him.'

Ballard looked beyond his young hired hand, and faced the deputy. Silas Layborne was a taller man, a few years older than Copper and heavier built. Ballard knew Layborne was a gruff kind of man, and proud. He provided trusty backing for Jefferson Kayte, and Ballard admired the qualities, considered him more than a tacit sidekick to the town's peace officer.

'What the hell's this all about, Silas?' Ballard asked of him.

'The kid comin' out with all this guff

about what he's done an' where he's done it. I've advised him, an' warned him not to, but he won't listen. I'm goin' to have to show him why he shouldn't.'

'It's a woman all right,' Ballard said with a slight shake of his head. The watchers were muttering more loudly, striving to keep the antagonism going. The excitement filled a gap in their lives, and they didn't want to be cheated out of it, not even by their employer.

'Yeah, that's right, Rube, it is a good one, too. Too damn good for the likes o' this toad, or for him to try an' sully her character.'

Ballard frowned in mild surprise, turned back to Copper. 'Sounds like you've been disrespectful, young Owen,' he said. 'Why? What's behind it?'

Copper railed instantly. 'Nothin'. Nothin' for him, anyways. Miss McSwane don't hardly know he exists, but he don't know it. Well, he ain't goin' to be the one who says who has her an' who don't.'

'Steady on there, Owen. You're making her sound like one of my brood mares.'

'Yeah, while he's got the grace of one o' your pack mules, an' she probably knows it,' Layborne snapped.

Ballard was suddenly keen to end the confrontation. He glanced at the other men, saw the palpable lust for a fight, the annoyance for him interfering.

'I'll give you three minutes,' he said, with a look down at his pocket-watch. 'That's long enough for your beef. When the time's up, Silas, you get yourself from my yard and don't come back until your thoughts are straight. Owen, win or lose, the matter's forgotten as long as you work here. Go on, get to it.'

The watching men grunted, looked at each other to confirm their approval.

Owen Copper, toughened by many hours of physical work, came in quickly. He was fired up, wanting to smack into Layborne right off. He caught the deputy with a looping right to the side

14

of the head, but then went too quickly forward. He was stopped by a short uppercut under the point of his jaw. His legs buckled and he swayed sideways, looking like he was going down. But Layborne missed with his second punch, swinging without damage past his head. Copper blinked, straightened and bored in. He caught Layborne with two short, fast swings to the side of the head, then another more powerful blow straight to the centre of the man's chest. Layborne staggered back. A cross pole of the pen hit him behind his legs, another high across his shoulder blades. It stopped him, prevented him from going down.

'Now's your chance, boy,' somebody shouted. 'He's got nowhere to go.'

Ballard looked furiously towards the man who spoke. 'I told you to get back to work, goddamn it. Next one to open his mouth gets the tip of my boot in it,' he rasped.

Layborne worked his way back to the center of the pen and landed a couple of meaty punches into Copper's body. He opened one of the youngster's eyebrows, in return found blood flowing freely from his own nose. Neither man gave ground, and for another full minute they slugged away, moving to the left, then to the right, trying to find a decisive punch.

They weren't hurting each other badly. The fight was fair enough, so Ballard didn't intervene. He was hoping they would continue to slam each other until he called time. With another minute to go, both men were bruised and bloody, breathing heavy but still on their feet. Ballard speculated what Miss McSwane would think. He knew a little of the new school teacher, but hadn't yet seen her, let alone been introduced. Most of the two weeks since her arrival he'd spent riding the brush country. When he returned, he'd been too exhausted to concern himself with meeting a town newcomer.

Copper sensed that Layborne was tiring. Summoning up fresh energy, he stomped in seeking to land the finishing punch. But it meant too much. He was over-anxious, and he walked straight into a bone-jarring blow. His head snapped back, giving Layborne a moment to spare in measuring out his next punch. He landed another heavy blow to the front of Copper's face, spreading the flow of blood that seeped from the youngster's gashed eyebrow. Now it was Layborne who sniffed a finish. He set himself for the lesson he wanted to mete out and moved forward.

'That's it,' Ballard shouted. 'You've had your round.'

There was an immediate grumble of protest, but Ballard's authority was overriding within the yards. He held out a hand towards Copper, lifted Layborne's gun belt from the gatepost and tossed it at him.

'I'd be grateful if you remembered what I said, Silas,' he reminded the deputy. 'Keep your private squabbles away from here. Owen, there's still work to do here before sundown.'

Ballard motioned the two other disgruntled stockmen to move off. He waited a moment before continuing with Layborne. 'With respect, Silas, perhaps young Owen had something. If you and *him* can't get it sorted, let the woman.'

Layborne wiped the crook of his arm across his face, then buckled on his gun belt. 'That's just fine with me, Rube. But he's the one with all the mouth.'

'Be that as it may, Silas, I don't want the upshot anywhere near my yard. You're the deputy sheriff, for god's sake, and right now Jeff Kayte's probably wondering where the hell you are.'

Layborne shot a quick glare at Copper who was at a trough pump, cleaning sweat and blood from his face, chest and arms. He swore under his breath and strode from the yard.

'That'll clear the air for a day or two. Until they meet next,' Tom Yurling said gleefully. 'Excellent match, those two.'

Ballard studied his yard manager for a moment. 'Yeah, well, let's get on,' he said. 'Entertainment don't salt the grits.'

Yurling grinned when he realized Ballard himself carried a small degree of pleasure in the scrap. He laughed cheerfully, turned away to harry the stockmen at their work.

Ballard returned to the store office. He flipped through some account sheets, stared distractedly at the previous week's paper work. He was still there an hour later when the first shadows of sundown fell across the yard. He was considering calling it a day when he heard the flat echo of two gun shots from closer in town.

'Deputy gone to shoot up the place,' he muttered as he turned the key in the door. He walked hurriedly to the tool room to see if his yard manager knew anything. 'Did you hear the gunfire?' he asked.

'Yeah. I'd guess Felix Shelter's place.'

'You know something, Tom?'

'Maybe. Accordin' to the mercantile fool, there's someone in there with a gun. Kayte's gone to sort it out. Probably nothin'.'

Ballard frowned. 'Nothing to do with Silas and young Owen, then?'

'Nope. Silas ain't that dumb, an' Owen's flat out on one of the pallets with his eyes shut.'

'What?'

'He's OK. Just too embarrassed to go home lookin' like a bear's dinner.'

Uncertain, and slightly troubled at what might be going on, Ballard went to the front of the yard. He stopped, waited beside the big latch-gate when he saw Milo Prentiss headed his way. Who needs the telegraph when you've got a Milo, he thought.

'What's up, Milo?' he called out, walking forward to meet the town's unofficial news carter.

'Sheriff Kayte's been killed.'

'Kayte?' Ballard questioned. 'Where? Who?'

'The saloon, an' his name's Noble.

Rites Noble, Mr Datch says. He's still there . . . just standin'. Mr Alton figures he's for makin' more trouble.'

'You mean Colvin Datch? How the hell's *he* involved?'

'He's not, Mr Ballard. He was at the jail.'

Tom Yurling cursed as he stepped between Ballard and Prentiss. 'Why'd you always come lookin' for Ruben? This trouble's not his, is it?' he snapped.

'I always do, Mr Yurlin'. An' Deputy Silas ain't around.' Prentiss looked uncertainly at Yurling, but Ballard put a reassuring hand to his shoulder.

'It's all right, I'll come, Milo,' he said, telling Yurling he might as well lock the yard for the night.

He was concerned right away that bigger trouble might be closing in. You don't go killing town sheriffs for nothing. The question was, who was going to react? If this man Noble was good enough to take down a sheriff like Kayte, then he could certainly dispatch

21

an affronted towner.

Ballard slowed momentarily as he crossed the street to the Shelter Saloon. There was a crowd already gathered, held back by uncertainty, the threat that lurked on the other side of the swing doors.

3

'You can take him, boy. It was him who killed our friend, Jefferson Kayte,' Colvin Datch said flatly.

'Goddamn it, Datch, you're throwin' your own kid up against a hired gunman,' Felix Shelter railed, as Bruno Datch stepped away from the bar counter.

Distancing himself from the customers, but considering Shelter's words, was the stranger Ruben Ballard immediately recognized as Rites Noble. Twenty feet away, lying face down was the body of the sheriff.

Also milling around were those from the street, those who had decided to follow Ballard into the saloon. Tom Yurling had run from the stockyard to join them.

'Just before the sheriff came down here, my boy an' me was in his office,'

Datch proclaimed. 'He said he'd give Bruno a chance an' let him carry a deputy's badge for a spell. Ain't exactly perfect timin', with Layborne not bein' here an' all, but what would be.'

The man was aware that his words surprised every person in the room. He turned to look directly at Noble, before continuing. 'Mister, you just shot dead a good lawman, but he was agein' an' tired out. Now let's see how you fare against an eager youngster who's settin' to prove himself.'

Ruben edged forward until he could see the protagonists more clearly.

Rites Noble was sparely built, had the look of a man who didn't make any sort of move without due consideration. 'My fight was with Kayte, so just take the boy out of here,' he told Datch. 'When I've taken me a drink, an' maybe some fixins' I'll move on. Hell, the only time I feel hungry enough to eat is after a shooting,' he added calmly.

Datch shook his head stubbornly. 'That ain't our way, mister. No one rides in, shoots our sheriff an' rides out again. My boy's takin' you on, empty gut or not.'

Bruno bit his lip, looked anxiously to his father.

'Hell, Rube, can you stop this? The man's gone loco,' Yurling said.

'Yeah. There's already been enough trouble,' Ruben replied, stepping closer to Datch. 'The law can handle this, Datch. There's enough testimony here to get it done right.'

'This ain't your business, Ballard,' Datch retorted sourly. 'Bruno's a deputy and willin' to earn a reputation as well as his corn.'

Ballard ignored Datch and looked to Felix Shelter. 'What happened, Felix? Did you see?'

'Yeah, reckon we all did,' Shelter said, thankful that Ruben Ballard was in his saloon, and ready to get something sorted. 'Noble sent word for Jeff to get down here. Sounds like he killed a friend of his a while ago . . . name o' Jewson. Jeff advised him to saddle and ride, but Noble wasn't having that. He stood his ground, called Jeff yellow. Jeff tried to take him, but he never had a flicker of a chance. Noble was ahead of any move.'

Rites Noble directed his interest to Ballard. 'Whoever the hell you are, feller, are you workin' for this town?' he said.

'Yeah, you could say that,' Ruben agreed. 'Sounds like what you did's not far off murder. Like Mr Datch here says, your way's not ours or anyone else's.'

Noble grinned daringly, while Datch moved towards his son. A moment later, Bruno nodded and stepped into the space that had gradually cleared.

'I'm sort o' deputized for the job,' he declared, calmly facing the gunman. 'You ain't goin' to let us arrest you, so we best get this over with.'

Ruben stepped forward, but Colvin Datch blocked his way. 'Keep the hell out o' this,' he snarled. 'Boy'll prove himself. You watch him.'

Datch's tiresome assurance angered Ruben. 'You want to see Bruno shot dead? Because that's what'll happen if we just stand and watch.'

'Hell, you all been worried about yourselves for too long. None o' you been takin' notice o' me an' my boy. He don't speak much for himself, but he ain't the pigeon you think. Certainly not to this cheap gun shark.'

For the first time, Rites Noble made a move. It was only slight, but it was a shift of unease. Suddenly, Bruno Datch was standing there confronting him, and the crowd were staying back. Ruben Ballard didn't look like he was going to intervene.

'I got to tell you good folk that, if it's *me* shot down, friends o' mine will hear about it, an' come to visit,' he warned. 'That's about all I got to say on the matter.' He turned to Bruno. 'So let's see how good you are, *pigeon*.'

The gunman hesitated for the shortest moment. Nothing moved, except the long muscles of his forearm as his

27

hand dropped to his Colt. Even as the crash of a single gunshot reverberated madly through the saloon, self-belief still showed in his rawboned features.

The onlookers had gathered tightly. They saw Bruno Datch pull his own Colt, in one, swift smooth movement, fire a bullet high into the front of Noble's narrow chest.

Noble staggered back on his heels. It was like a drunken dance step, a movement the man couldn't remember and he fired down to the saw-dusted floor in frustration. Then, without a sound he bent forward, collapsed and died.

'Hell, he did it,' Felix Shelter muttered. 'Kid shot him dead.'

'Yeah, I saw.' Tom Yurling was studying the blank expression of Bruno Datch with sudden, puzzling awareness.

Colvin Datch motioned for Shelter to pour him a drink. He downed it in one and handed the glass back. 'I'd stand one for Bruno, but he ain't reached majority,' he humoured and twisted a wry grin. He turned to the crowd behind him. 'But you can see why Jefferson Kayte was interested,' he said. 'You're never too young to start learnin', was one o' the last things the man conceded. All you folks got to do now is support his proposal an' pin some tin on my boy.'

Tom Yurling looked quickly at Ruben, together with most of the other customers. Ruben was considering what some folk can make up from very little. In Bruno Datch's case it was nothing more than the ability to shoot a man; for himself, it was a business standing, the faculty to string more than two words together, maybe a level of nerve.

'Nothing's going to detract from your boy's prowess with a gun, Datch . . . what he just did,' he started. 'But that doesn't mean we have a new deputy. It's not Bonachon's way. Normally we get to vote on those kind of matters, as you rightly know.'

'Yeah, I know, smartass. You forgettin' what Noble said about his friends?

Are you goin' to wait an' see how many of 'em are close by? For chris'sake, swear Bruno in now. Unless you got somethin' personal against him?'

Datch's comment seemed to hang in the air, holding the onlookers to continued silence.

'I've got nothing more and nothing less than anyone else here, Datch.'

'An' you agree he's got the ability for the job?'

'Unless the boy's got hidden depths, no, I don't think I do,' Ruben offered a look at Bruno. 'How old is he, seventeen . . . eighteen? I'd ask *him*, only right now it looks like his mind's on something else. Besides, you're obviously the one with the mouth.'

'Yeah, you're a smartass all right, Ballard. But right now that don't matter. Believe me, Bruno's a man full grown with all his faculties, an' Jeff Kayte went along with that. So, as you ain't yet runnin' this town, I reckon it's other folk . . . some of 'em, gathered here . . . who can decide what kind o' man they want to protect 'em.'

Something warned Ruben to be wary of Bruno Datch. He'd heard enough to know the man wasn't kindly disposed to the law, although he couldn't think of one person who had anything specific on him, or could make an accusation.

'I'd go along with that. And there's no reason to suppose I'm going to influence them,' he replied. 'I just reckon Bruno's too young ... too inexperienced for a deputy's job.'

Datch was becoming impatient and his breathing got heavier. 'The thing is, Ballard, Bruno's here, an' Layborne's not. What the hell's *that* got to do with experience? As for his age, I say, if you're good enough, you're old enough. With half the town's peace keepin' force lyin' dead at your feet, what do you say to that?'

As his name was mentioned, Silas Layborne came through the swing doors. He carried his hat, his head still wet from dunking himself under one of the stockyard water pumps. He had heard the shooting from the saloon, earlier, but expecting Kayte to be on hand, had decided to go to the jailhouse and change his messed up clothes. It was while he was considering an explanation for what he'd been up to, that he'd heard about Kayte getting shot by a gunfighter.

Now, confronted by Kayte's body outstretched on the floor, a stranger's body beside it, Layborne cursed, threw a questioning look at Ruben Ballard and Tom Yurling. 'I can see what the hell happened, but how . . . why?' he rasped.

Yurling shrugged, shook his head. 'This hired gunfighter named Noble rode in an' shot down Jeff. Young Bruno here then took Noble. Be splittin' hairs to say it was anythin' but fair. Upshot is though, Silas, an' accordin' to Bruno's pa, we now got to decide what lawmen to have.'

'Accordin' to Bruno's pa?' Layborne echoed incredulously.

'Yeah, an' decision's already made,' Colvin Datch put in quickly. 'You get to be sheriff, Layborne, an' my boy gets to be your deputy. That'll be for a short while, o' course. The way Sheriff Kayte saw it.'

Layborne took a lingering look at the dead sheriff. 'I reckon it's the way *you're* seein' it, mister,' he said thoughtfully. 'He never mentioned me gettin' any sort o' help.'

'Well, he would've if you'd been around, Deputy. Now, seein' as Bruno's just proved himself in front of you all, there shouldn't be any problem. Let's trust you an' him can prove yourselves as good as the outgoin'.'

'With him lying dead at our feet, that's a good line in irony,' Ruben muttered.

4

Silas Layborne was fittingly shocked by Kayte's dramatic death, dismayed by the proposal for young Bruno Datch to be his legally deputized sidekick. He had on occasion mentioned the youngster as someone who should be watched. Bruno appeared to be easily influenced, not by his peers whom he stayed well clear of, but solely by his father. And Layborne's suspicions were whetted by Kayte, who curiously, never had much of an opinion about Colvin Datch.

Layborne walked across to have a close look at his friend and former sheriff. Placing a hand on the man's shoulder, a deep feeling of sorrow gripped him. He couldn't yet take on board the fact that Kayte wouldn't ever again be there to support or cheer him. He cursed everything as he straightened, fought back the pain as his eyes sought Bruno Datch.

'You should have left shootin' Noble to me, you freak punk,' he rasped bitterly. 'Despite what's goin' on here, an' until we've had a proper burial, I'll act as temporary sheriff. Right now, some o' you help me get him back to the jailhouse.'

Ruben Ballard moved forward with Tom Yurling. Together, they lifted Kayte's body, and carried it past Colvin Datch. Bruno Datch remained standing back. Now he was watching his father, seemingly uncertain what to say or what to do with himself.

When the three men had exited the saloon, Colvin Datch swallowed a second shot of whiskey.

'Mr Shelter,' he said. 'Bein' an upstandin' citizen, knows an' known by most everyone in this town, I'm puttin' it to you, that my boy handled himself real well here today?'

Felix Shelter offered no more than a hesitant nod of agreement. 'Was more like Noble he handled. But yeah, I understand what you're sayin'. So what?'

'I reckon we should more fully recognize it . . . fill in the hole we got. We should make this situation a lesser one.'

Shelter looked unsure, looked around the room for support. A ranch hand looking as though he wanted to say something caught his eye.

'I never seen a boy his age act like that,' the man stated. 'If his pa here wants him kickin' his heels outside the jailhouse for a spell, he'll get no argument from me, an' I don't suppose anyone else. But, I must say, if it was any kin o' mine, I'd be lookin' for a job with longer-lastin' prospects,' he added after a quick look to where the sheriff had fallen.

Datch looked around, searching faces to see most men nod in conformity. 'I guess some men are born to live a long life treadin' cattle dirt,' he said. 'Then there's those who turn it into the sod. Some even aspire to sellin' nails an' biscuits behind a shop counter. But my boy's only ever wanted to be a lawman . . . standin' up for the rights of others.'

'Takin' that office isn't the only way to achieve success,' Shelter suggested.

'It's a wish, goddamn it. *His* wish, an' you've no right to stop him,' Datch snapped. 'Hell, I'm just askin' you to give him the chance he's earned.' With that, Datch motioned Bruno to stand alongside him. They didn't speak, just watched what happened around them, listened as best they could to the talk.

Five minutes later, Ruben Ballard, Tom Yurling and Silas Layborne returned. Datch instantly called a get-together. His proposal was Silas Layborne for Sheriff and Bruno Datch for Deputy.

'Unauthorized an' out of order, but I don't know about illegal,' Layborne muttered.

'Yeah. I doubt it'll stop 'em putting a hand in the air. What happens then?' Yurling asked.

'Silas gets a pet assassin for his deputy,' Ruben answered. 'Maybe it's the healthier outcome. I mean, you wouldn't want him *against* you.'

Bruno Datch stood beside his father, saying nothing. He was now tied into the idea as though he'd supported and proposed himself.

'So what do you reckon, Rube?' Layborne prompted. 'We all know the town looks to you for advice.'

'Every man here can speak for himself,' Colvin Datch interjected. 'It ain't right my boy gets penalized 'cause of one man's goddamn bugbear.'

Ruben turned on Datch. 'No, and it ain't right that he gets elected to office because of his goddamn shooter and his father's menace,' he retaliated. 'I'm agreeing with Silas Layborne for sheriff, but that's it. No one's making me decide further.'

'I'll go along with that,' Tom Yurling joined in. His words were quickly echoed by one or two others, but some of Felix Shelter's customers shuffled to the other end of the room. They were in doubt, or fearful or both.

Datch glowered as he realized that any support for his boy was waning. 'So what about you, Felix Shelter? Are you sayin' Bruno ain't worth a chance? On approval, even?'

Shelter suddenly found himself speaking for his customers. 'I got nothin' against your son, Datch. Not a thing,' he started, honestly. 'But hell . . . his age . . . I mean . . . '

'A boy can stand his ground as good . . . maybe *better* than some men.'

'Yeah, if he's holdin' a gun. But otherwise?'

'Hell, we all have to start somewhere . . . sometime?'

Shelter looked around to see that Ruben Ballard was watching Bruno Datch intently. The stockyard owner's mind was obviously working on something, but his face was expressionless.

'Put like that, maybe we can try him for a bit,' Shelter offered.

There was a rumble of assent, and

Datch quickly and expediently endorsed Layborne's role as sheriff.

This time, men raised their hands into the heady, smoke-filled air. There was no need for a count, but it was noticeable that not everyone was in agreement with such a rough-and-ready election.

'Good, so now we can nominate Bruno,' Datch continued, lifting his own hand.

Felix Shelter was already committed, as were those who were now moving closer to the bar. Ruben and Yurling made no move to appoint Bruno, nor did a couple of their stockyard workers. It was clear, however, that the young Datch was being chosen as Layborne's deputy sheriff.

Wearing a proud grin, Colvin Datch pushed in to the crowded bar. He was satisfying the wily customers who were already relishing a celebration drink, and called for drinks all round.

Ruben Ballard and Yurling stepped out onto the boards. They were soon accompanied by a troubled Silas Layborne.

'It's not good, Rube. You can't run a town like this,' the newly chosen sheriff said thickly. 'Those punters . . . good folk though they might be . . . have been railroaded.'

'We all went along with it, Silas,' Ruben replied. 'It was a vote of sorts, and too late now. I think you'll make out fine. Just have him walk in front of you when it gets dark.'

'Huh, funny. Remember, you're the one's he's goin' to remember didn't support him.'

Ruben and Yurling smiled thinly. They stepped down into the street and without further conversation, returned to the stockyards.

In his office again, Ruben asked Yurling what it was he had on his mind.

'What do you think?'

'While he's influenced by Silas, not his pa, I'm thinking maybe Bruno will make out all right.'

Yurling shook his head. 'It's a tad late

in the year for maybes, Rube. But it's not so much about him. You know as well as I do it's Colvin Datch who's up to something. Who the hell would want to sell his own kid out an' why?'

Ruben nodded. '*Him*, obviously, and Silas can figure out why. But *I've* got a business to take care of, and I'm heading out to see Tedstone.'

'Meantime, town slides back to bein' lawless,' Yurling flipped back.

Ruben looked irritated. 'What's that supposed to mean? Right or wrong, I thought we all agreed on what happened back there.'

'You could have said more against young Bruno, feelin' as you do.'

'Hell, Tom, there was nothing more I could have done. Time will prove it one way or another. That's the way it is.'

'Yeah,' Yurling growled. 'So when Datch makes his move, we'll just let him get on with it?'

'What the hell do you think he's after . . . his long game?'

'Don't know. Not yet, anyways. It's

obviously not his son's welfare he's seekin'.'

For a long moment Ruben held Yurling's stare, his thoughts. Then he grunted in exasperation, shrugged and went out into the yard. As full dark settled across the town, he rode south from the yards, then west towards the San Rafael foothills.

5

It was nine o'clock, and after the violent, eventful day, Ruben was seriously wondering whether he could run his business from out of town. Buy himself a pair of army-surplus campaign tents, fetch up by flowering bluebonnet on Grapevine Creek. *Just half a goddamn chance*, he was thinking as he reached the Tedstone spread. He thought he'd see the ranch house well lit as it usually was, and Jake Tedstone always kept a light outside one of his home barns. 'There's a light in the window for those who look,' as the rancher liked to say.

Pondering on the relative darkness, Ruben reined in outside the house. The first thing he heard was the lilt of a woman's laughter, and with keener interest, he stepped slowly up onto the broad veranda.

Jake Tedstone was a widower, father of two young girls. Ruben knew that since his wife's death, the man hadn't so much as glanced at another woman. The front door was partly open. To Ruben it was a further sign of no furtive activity beyond, but he stopped to listen for a moment.

'You don't say? An' right in front o' you?' he heard Tedstone asking.

'Yes, he literally fell at my feet. You can imagine the shock. The first man in . . . to speak to me . . . well, almost. I thought he was dead.'

'An' what happened then?'

'Deputy Layborne just dragged him away. He came back and apologized. Said the man didn't mean any harm. He'd had too much to drink, apparently.'

The woman's voice was as composed and refined as Ruben had heard in a long while. Instinctively, he knew who she was. And it wasn't just the mention of Silas Layborne's name.

'Well, if it's who I think it is, that's

one big degree of muchness, ma'am,' Tedstone said. 'I once seen an old soldier staggerin' along blind drunk, complainin' he'd finished off Shelter's liquid stock. Hah, he had both hands stuck out in front of him, graspin' for a bottle, until he tripped over the mercantile dog. We rolled him into the alley to sober up, an' he stayed there until his sister found him the followin' mornin'.'

The man's ensuing laughter rolled from the house out into the darkness, and Ruben gave a tight smile. Satisfied he wouldn't startle an intruder, or worse, he stepped into the house. To his left, through an inner doorway he saw a big man pitching backwards and forwards in his rocker. Facing him sat a woman with a head of fair hair that fell straight to her shoulders.

He coughed his arrival, rattling his knuckles against the door as he stepped forward.

Tedstone's face lifted, the laughter eased and he waved Ruben in. 'Ruben.

Hell, man, the doors are open.'

'Yeah, they are. Your lights are down, though.' Ruben walked on into the room and the woman half turned to face him. She started to smile, and, for the shortest moment, Ruben thought it was the reaction of recognizing someone, then swiftly deciding you didn't want them to know it.

'You two must have met,' Tedstone said easily. 'No need for me to make one o' them formal introductions.'

'No,' they both answered with a slight shake of their heads.

'Not met? Well, well.' Tedstone gave a quizzical look, held one open hand towards the young lady, the other towards Ruben. 'Grace McSwane an' Ruben Ballard. Schoolmistress an' stockman,' he announced, looking from one to the other. 'I guess that covers the essentials.'

Grace McSwane nodded calmly. Ruben did the same.

'Maybe I have an advantage,' he started. 'Bonachon's not exactly a big town, the arrival of a new school ma'am is news. But seeing you now, I'd understand if other qualities created the attention.'

'Other qualities, Mr Ballard? And what might those be?' she queried.

In Ruben's experience, only someone stupid or self-assured asks a question to which they already know the answer, or don't care about. And Grace McSwane certainly wasn't possessed of the former quality. 'Nothing of any import,' he said, recalling what it was that young Owen Copper had bragged about.

He pulled a chair away from the wall, sat down and accepted a glass of brandy offered him by Tedstone.

'Miss McSwane came out to see about the girls an' their attendin' school next year,' Tedstone said. 'She's come up with a fine idea. An idea that all of us out this way will appreciate.'

Ruben smiled. 'I hope that doesn't include me.'

'No, Mr Ballard. I'm sure you live in

town,' Grace McSwane replied, returning the smile. 'Living out here has many advantages, but for a child and their schooling, so much time is wasted every day in traveling. Wearisome, too, and inconvenient.'

'So what's the answer? You have one?'

'Maybe. I've suggested to Mr Tedstone that we build a place in town where children from outlying ranches can stay over. Say for three nights a week, then go home for long weekends.'

'There are such boarding schools, I hear. But this isn't New York or New England. How about the running . . . the financing?' Momentarily, Ruben thought that was where *he* came in. Then he remembered it was his idea to ride out to see Jake Tedstone.

'Well, I'll supervise the boarding, and I'm sure there won't be a shortage of helpers once we're established. As far as finance is concerned, it's a case of expediency . . . where the interest lies. Parents could donate food or money . . . whatever suits them.'

'Sure thing,' Tedstone cut in, enthusiastically. 'Nobody's goin' short o' beef, Ruben, that's for certain. As for the other truck, George Stillman's already said he's in favour, an' he's a farmer. Others can give what Miss McSwane thinks is appropriate. I can't see a problem. Where there's a will, an' all that.'

Ruben gave a slight shrug. 'It seems to me a fair old task,' he said with obvious reserve.

'So one worth doing well, Mr Ballard,' Grace McSwane said quickly. 'Besides, if I'm to be effective in Bonachon, it's the only way. You have doubts about my capability?'

'Nope. I just reckon you'll need more than a proposal with meat an' taters, ma'am.' With that, Ruben turned to Tedstone. 'I'd like to head back tonight, Jake. There's trouble, and I want to keep an eye on things . . . the stock,' he said.

Feeling there was a slight undercurrent of tension, Tedstone frowned. He

50

knew by Ruben's manner there was something else on his mind; from personal experience, the more you have the more you got to lose.

'Trouble? Somethin's happened in town?' he asked.

'Yeah, today. Jeff Kayte got himself killed by a gunfighter. An incident that dated back a year or so, apparently. I could have, maybe *should* have told you first off. The right moment's not always there, I guess.'

'Jeez, Ruben. Anything else?'

'Bruno Datch took the gunfighter out.'

'Goddamn. Colvin Datch's boy? The kid?'

'Yeah, him. Silas was elected sheriff.'

'How the hell did all this happen?'

'Datch milked the situation. He plumped for Bruno as deputy, and customers of the Shelter voted the boy in . . . sort of.'

'You sure you want to stay in town?' Tedstone said, turning to Grace McSwane.

'I don't suppose it's always like this.'

'No, it's not. Jefferson Kayte was one o' the best lawmen there is. He was that mix of tough an' tolerant, an' he had my respect. Layborne was makin' out real good, too. Hell, ma'am, it's hardly ever like this.'

'I thought town sheriffs got elected by town councils,' Grace McSwane said.

'Yes, they do. But from what Ruben says, it sounds like we've had some sort o' shotgun vote. Silas might make out, but I'm not so sure. I'm guessin' Ruben thinks the same. The boy Datch is a strange cove, an' his pa ain't someone you'd want to pledge your faith with. Sorry, I'm not paintin' much of a picture, am I?'

Grace McSwane shook her head with uncertainty. 'What's the alternative if the mindful people of the town aren't in accord with what's happened?'

'It doesn't matter much whether they are or not,' Ruben answered. 'The election, if you can call it that, has been made. Layborne's accepted the position and some of those mindful folk have decided to risk it with Bruno Datch. That's the long and the short of it, and until the end of the year, I don't think it's going to get changed. Anyway, Jake, with regard to the business I came to see you about, I'd like to get it done, if you don't mind.'

'Yeah, that's all right, Ruben.' Tedstone got to his feet and indicated that Grace McSwane should help herself to more coffee. 'It's not that any of us regards a man's life as cheap, Miss McSwane . . . Grace, but sometimes life an' business has to move along,' he said thoughtfully. 'Me an' Ruben's got one or two things to take care of, so if you hear anythin' from the girls' room, will you just look in on 'em? We won't be long.'

Grace nodded and watched the two men leave the room. She was vaguely miffed by Ruben's manner, couldn't see how or why he was so lukewarm towards her schooling idea. As she poured herself another cup of coffee, she had the impression he was already kicking up a low hurdle. She sat quietly considering her plans, knowing she would need the encouragement and help of men like Ruben Ballard. It was plain he was good at business, a man she thought would understand all the benefits her boarding school would bring. But now she couldn't see how to approach him as a likely benefactor. She was annoyed because she'd let an ideal opportunity slip through her fingers.

A half hour later, Tedstone extended his hand to Ruben. 'It's settled then with half up front,' he said. 'You'll arrange for the timber haulage, an' balance is payable when the buildin's done.'

'Agreed,' Ruben said. After a final scan of the figures, he slipped a small account book and pencil back in his pocket and picked up his hat.

'I reckon our little deal's been taken care of, too, Grace,' Tedstone said.

'Ruben's headin' back to town, so you can ride together. You never know when there's a bear or coyote waitin' on the trail.'

Grace McSwane looked pensively up at Ruben. 'If Mr Ballard doesn't mind my company.'

'I doubt there's any danger of me minding that,' Ruben replied.

'Good.' Grace McSwane stood and collected her handbag. 'For the sake of appearance, you can drive,' she added with an inscrutable smile.

Tedstone followed them out through the front door onto the broad verandah. He waited cheerfully as Ruben brought Grace McSwane's rig around front, said how well the evening had gone as Ruben tied in his mare on a long rein.

'Don't let him ruffle your feathers, miss,' he said. 'Jeff Kayte's death will have troubled him. Ruben's a good man, always given his support to Kayte an' the law. He'll be feelin' the loss more'n a lot of us.'

Grace McSwane didn't answer, but

she took the sentiment in as she stepped into the rig. She gave a light smile, sat next to Ruben.

'Two weeks, Jake,' Ruben called out as he swung the rig around.

'Drive easy. You got a cultured load up there,' the rancher answered back.

6

Grace McSwane was curiously surprised at the way Ruben handled the rig. He negotiated the rocks and ruts, the rise and fall of the trail with such ease and smoothness, she didn't think it could be the same route she had taken earlier.

They travelled at a good rate, and once on the main trail, Ruben gave the horse more of its head on the way back to town. It was a clear night and a cool wind whipped gently in their faces.

'This is just about how I imagined it to be,' Grace McSwane said. 'So quiet with the stars looking almost within reach.'

Ruben looked skyward, silently nodding his agreement. 'I think first names would be more appropriate, certainly more agreeable,' he said. 'And yes. Sometimes you can top a bluff, and think you're going to push your head right in amongst them. The stars, that is.'

Grace smiled easily. She watched him as he drove the rig, his awareness familiar and natural. 'Was the sheriff a good friend, Ruben?' she asked.

'Yes, he was. And a good man.'

Grace felt she was somehow intruding on Ruben's thoughts. But, mindful of Jake Tedstone's words about life going on, and not knowing when she would get another chance, she continued. 'How can a stranger just ride into town and kill like that? Surely there are laws? Common sense says it's wrong.'

Ruben shuffled uneasily, went on looking straight ahead. 'There's no law that says it can't happen. When Jeff Kayte pinned on the badge, he knew what he was doing. Noble was a challenge to civil liberties, and he couldn't back down on that. If he did, others like him would have ridden roughshod over ordinary, peaceable folk.'

'So he was killed rising to a challenge? That's ridiculous.'

'It's ridiculous to think *that*, after what I just said,' Ruben replied testily. 'If anyone doesn't agree with the town's organization, they usually ride on.'

'And quite obviously you didn't.'

'No. I did what I thought was right for me. Always have done,' he said, and Grace heard sternness.

'Are you thinking you could have done more to help your friend? Would that have been right? Your staying was to no avail?'

Ruben turned towards Grace and his features hardened. 'Yes, I think I could have done more . . . something. Probably not the only one, either. If we don't ride on, we decide to stay and live by laws and statutes. Paradoxically, it's that what kills us, if in the meantime we don't get pushed under.'

'And this Bruno Datch has ridden roughshod through all that? From what I understood, he's improved his community status *and* been elected a deputy sheriff. Isn't it a tad inconsistent, formal guidelines for some?'

'Datch just got there first. That caused the problem,' Ruben said, his manner forcing Grace to look away hurriedly. She sensed the disappointment, knew she had overstepped the line.

'I'm sorry, my view is uncalled for,' she offered quietly.

'No matter,' he told her and flicked the horse into a run.

For a time, Grace was uncomfortable with the speed, let alone the risk of being bumped from her seat. But she made no mention of it until they had levelled out on the flats approaching town.

'Well, that part of the journey was quite exhilarating. What is it you don't approve of?' she asked. 'Why do I upset you so?'

Ruben studied her for a long moment. 'What makes you think I am?'

'The last ten minutes of this drive. But from the moment we were introduced, I've sensed your antipathy. If I've offended you, Ruben, I'd like to know how. You can tell me that, surely.'

Ruben sought the words to deal with Grace's question. She was right and he knew the reason for his coolness. 'There was some trouble at my place today,' he came out with.

Grace stared curiously at him. 'Right, I see. But how do I figure in that?'

Ruben was silent for another long moment. 'It was a fist fight between Silas Layborne and Owen Copper. According to one of them, they were fighting for the right to woo you. I'm no expert, but in a town like this, that sort of trouble can be very dangerous. It's not like there was a surplus of eligible women.'

'That's not my fault,' Grace blurted out. 'I haven't given either one of them due cause. It's nonsense to suggest otherwise.'

'Beating the stuffing out of each other isn't nonsense. You must have known they were rivals for your attention.'

The colour drained from Grace's face. She stared silently down at her hands, and Ruben could feel the emotion welling up inside her.

Ten minutes later, he pulled the rig alongside the steps of the Bonachon boarding house. Grace climbed down before she said anything.

'I did ask, and you told me,' she said. 'Now if you'll allow me a moment to explain. It wasn't what I was expecting, but perhaps that is my fault. I'm truly sorry that it's come to this but, believe me, the only sort of encouragement I've given any man here is by answering when I'm spoken to. If I'm to be accepted in this town and to further myself, what else should I do? I'm very surprised that either of them feels I'm worth fighting over, and I will rectify it as soon as possible. Hopefully, it will avert more trouble for you and your business. Good night, Ruben.'

Without a backwards glance, Grace went on into the foyer of the house.

Ruben shook his head, allowed the words and thoughts to settle. 'And goodnight to you, Miss McSwane. I'll be taking the rig back then,' he muttered sarcastically. He was in no doubt about the sincerity of the new schoolmistress, but then nor did he doubt it of the two men fighting. He cursed and moved the rig on for the livery stable.

At the far end of town, Ruben hauled in under the lamp outside the wide, open doors.

The livery man who had obviously been waiting for somebody or something, stomped out to meet him.

'Rube, where you been?' he said agitatedly. 'You heard the news? Where's the school ma'am?'

'Miss McSwane's at the boarding house. What news do you mean?'

'Silas is dead. Been another killin'.'

Ruben cursed again, much stronger. 'Someone's brought a goddamn hex to this town,' he rasped. 'Look after the mare. I'll take the rig on to the yard.'

Ruben stared at Tom Yurling for a long, considerate moment. 'What the hell's happening, Tom?'

'I don't know, Rube. I don't think anybody does at the moment. All I know is, Silas was found dead behind the jailhouse, an' Bruno Datch is holdin' Owen for murder.'

'Owen?' Ruben muttered in amazement. He peered intently in the direction of the jailhouse where he could see a small crowd milling in the street. 'Get in, Tom,' he said.

As soon as the rig drew to a halt outside the jailhouse, Ruben was down and onto the boardwalk. He didn't speak to or catch the eye of any of the expectant eager townsfolk. He went straight into the office, finding Felix Shelter looking troubled, and Colvin Datch standing beside the sheriff's desk. Why the hell aren't I surprised, he thought.

Bruno Datch was further back,

outside a cell that was holding Owen Copper. The youngster stood close up against the bars, his face pallid in the light cast from a single, hanging oil lamp.

'Whatever you got on your mind, Ballard, can it,' Colvin Datch said angrily as soon as Ruben appeared. 'We all got this thing under control. We've even given a bulletin to them who's interested.'

Ruben ignored him and looked hard at the man's son. 'What happened here?' he demanded. 'At this moment, Bruno, you're the person in charge.'

Bruno Datch looked quickly towards his father who nodded grimly. 'OK, boy, just tell him. Then I'll stay here with you keepin' guard,' the man said.

Bruno knew Ruben as a hard and determined man, someone he had a sneaky regard for, albeit a distant one. In particular, he liked the way Ruben's friends acted towards him, the friendly respect. Like most other townsfolk, Bruno had heard rumours concerning

Ruben's past. But even his father had given that short shrift, saying that everyone had them. Ruben Ballard was a man who had success, built his stock business without help from anybody.

'I heard a shot after Layborne — the sheriff, that is — went out to check on the horses,' Bruno started his explanation. 'I ran out, but he was already on his knees. Copper was running towards the alley an' I put out a shot to stop him. An' it did. When I saw the sheriff was dead, I brought him inside. Pa came, an' then we saw he didn't have a gun.'

'He didn't have a gun? So how the hell did he shoot Silas?'

'The gun was amongst the bins. Pa went back an' found it with one bullet fired. We put him in a cell. Pa says it'll go to trial quick.'

'Like his election, eh, Bruno — '

'Listen, Ballard,' Colvin Datch interrupted. 'While Bruno was takin' care of a killer an' a threat to this town, we learned that Layborne an' Copper were hand-to-hand fightin' in one o' your stock pens. So with Copper already implicatin' himself, are you goin' to argue against holdin' him, because he's one o' your own cavvy men?'

Ruben smiled coldly and swore at Datch. He went to the cell and nodded at Copper. 'Did you do what they're sayin', Owen?' he asked.

Copper shook his head emphatically. 'Hell, boss, why'd you ask? Sure I was sour but I don't really know why I ran. Some sort o' scared, I guess. I knew how bad it would look.'

Ruben shook his head. 'What were you doing anywhere near the jailhouse?'

Copper gripped the cell bars tight with intensity. He turned to look across at where Silas Layborne's body lay outstretched under a blanket in the adjoining cell.

'I figured on getting settled with Miss McSwane,' he answered quietly. 'I waited a bit, then went to find her, but she was out of town.'

Ruben knew that part of the story

was true and he nodded.

'I know it doesn't make sense but I went lookin' for Silas instead. When I saw him at the jailhouse, Bruno Datch was there, so I waited until he came out on his own. I saw him going for the back door, so I ran around to cut him off.'

'Well, you sure managed that, you murderous little skunk,' Colvin Datch snapped.

'I didn't kill anybody,' Copper shouted defiantly.

'Well, I'm sayin' he did,' Datch continued. 'An' I'm sayin' Bruno proved his worth once again, an' deserves recognition. Right now we got ourselves a little gallows bird here, an' tomorrow we'll get him oven ready.'

'I'm beginning to think you've got something else in mind, Datch,' Ruben said. 'Why are you so keen? If justice or even civic development was involved, you might just have to prove something before talking about such a penalty.'

'We've got a prisoner to watch,

Ballard. Just concern yourself with that. We'll hear everybody's side tomorrow.'

Ruben gave Datch a long, threatening look before stepping in closer to Copper. 'Remember, only the truth, Owen,' he said calmly. 'Meantime, go over exactly what you saw happen. Just concern yourself with that, and don't worry about anything else. I'm standing by you.'

'They're already double-dealin', boss. It's for Bruno to come out good. I got no chance unless more'n you believe me.'

'It's good enough for now, Owen. Believe *that*. Go and lie down. Stay out of it.' Walking away, Ruben almost shouldered aside Colvin and Bruno Datch. He looked at them and shaped a chilly smile. 'Anything happens to that boy, you'll both die. That's a promise,' he warned quietly.

On the boardwalk, half a dozen men started asking questions. Ruben strode around them, said how they should listen for news the coming daybreak.

He crossed the street, waved for Tom Yurling to bring the rig over.

Back in the yard, Ruben asked Yurling to ready-up a horse for him.

'Sure. But where the hell are you goin' this time o' night?' Yurling asked.

'Somebody's got to tell the Coppers. One or two of them will want to be here or hereabouts.'

Yurling nodded in agreement. 'Yeah. If only to start takin' the jail apart. But it's best you stay, Rube. So I'll go,' he decided. 'How do you rate young Owen's chances? They'll want to know that.'

Ruben thought about it for a moment. 'Tell them the truth, that you don't know. Bring them in, but don't tell them it's bad for Owen if anyone accepts the Datch version of what happened.'

'Hell, no.' Yurling cursed and went to get a horse from their saddle stock.

Ruben stood in the dark, glad he didn't have to make the ride out to the Copper place. Worried what would happen after sun-up, he walked slowly across the big yard. For a few hours he would make use of the pallet on the floor under the worktable in his stores office.

7

The courthouse hearing took place in the saloon. Felix Shelter was only too happy to charge the County ten times more than he'd make from a morning selling beer and whiskey. The main room was packed to capacity an hour before Justice Billy Vane took his seat and rapped a shot glass for attention.

Vane had high standing among the town's business men. He had personal wealth of such significance; corrupt, illegal payments held little influence.

Deputy Bruno Datch was standing behind the seated Owen Copper. Across from him, Colvin Datch was looking confident at the day's possibilities.

Ruben Ballard stood inside the side doorway, watching Owen Copper. Five minutes earlier, he reminded the youngster that although his experience in these matters was limited, he would speak up for him when required.

'Let's get on with it,' Vane said loudly. The moment there was silence in the room, he started proceedings in a calculated, intolerant voice. 'Officer of law can make his charge, then we'll hear the response. Carry on.'

Bruno Datch stepped forward. He chewed his bottom lip, looked anxiously at his father.

'Tell it straight, boy,' Colvin Datch said. 'There's nothin' to fear. It weren't you who shot Layborne dead.'

Vane pushed a superfluous legal tome to one side, smacked his shot glass hard down on the table in front of him. 'Anyone prompting or making behaviours I don't like, I'll have 'em thrown out. Get on with it, Deputy Datch.'

Bruno shifted a step forward. 'Well, sir, it's just like I said before. I was hearin' out Silas ... Mr Layborne, about what duties I'd be carryin' out as a deputy. He laughed a bit, said it would be the last time he'd be takin' the trash out. Then he said that was it for the day, and he was soon for the land of Nod. He went out back, an' almost at the same time, there was a gunshot. One loud gunshot.'

'And you were on your own at the time? Just you and Sheriff Layborne?' Vane asked.

'Yessir. When I went out to see what was goin' on, I saw Owen Copper. He was running towards the fence, back o' the yard where the cans are. I didn't know who it was at first, there's no lights out there. I shot over his head, an' yelled for him to stop. I guess I was close enough for him to know I'd plug him easy if he didn't.'

'Yes, I've heard of your prowess with a hand gun, Mr Datch. Perhaps he'd heard the same,' Vane cut in. 'What happened next?'

'I brought him into the jailhouse, sir.'

Vane nodded thoughtfully, looked up to quell the murmuring. 'And then?' he prompted.

'My pa came in from the street, an'

74

asked what all the shootin' was about. I told him I wasn't sure, an' we put Copper in a cell. Pa carried a lantern out into the yard, an' we found Mr Layborne. He was layin' between the trash cans. He'd been shot in the back. There was nothin' we could do for him.'

Vane gave Colvin Datch a hard unsettling stare. 'Just out of curiosity, what were you doing there?' he asked.

'Keepin' an eye on my boy. Nothin' so wrong in that, is there? It was his first night on duty.'

'Hmm, don't we know it,' Vane muttered, looking around the provisional courtroom as though for agreement. He hammered again for silence. 'You take instructions from me, not your pa or anyone else in this room. You understand?' he directed as Bruno looked to his father once again.

'Yes, sir. But there ain't that much more to tell.'

'Tell us about the gunshot you heard. Presumably there was a gun,' Vane said.

'Yessir, there was. But when we brought Mr Layborne inside, Pa saw he didn't have it, so we went outside to look. It must have been underneath his body, an' Pa showed that one bullet had been fired. Some people started to arrive then, an' Pa told 'em we'd taken in Owen Copper. That's about it, sir.'

Another rumble of voices moved through the room. From behind the bar, Felix Shelter was considering his sales of whiskey when proceedings were done. Ruben continued his silent stance leaning against the side wall, wondering where the deliberations would take them.

Grace McSwane came in, and saw him. The look she gave was one of resignation that any sort of trial hearing was going to harm her reputation. He held her attention until she sat down. A moment later, Billy Vane was calling his name.

'Mr Ballard, I understand you're here to represent Owen Copper. If that's so, let's hear what the plea's going to be.'

'Not guilty,' Ruben said sternly.

'How the hell can you claim that after what I told you last night an' this mornin?' Colvin Datch retorted angrily. 'You callin' me an' an elected lawman liars?'

'One more outburst from you, Datch, and I'll have you thrown out for disturbing the peace, whether you're a witness or not,' Vane snapped back.

Colvin Datch scowled. He had rubbed shoulders with Billy Vane on a few occasions, but never for anything more social, a drink or business discussion. It rankled somewhat because Vane held trespass rights to land which Datch occasionally and with permission, used to transport goods to the overland trail out of San Bernardino.

'Call your witnesses,' Vane requested of Bruno.

Without being asked, Colvin Datch took his place alongside Vane. He glared sourly, but Vane ignored him.

When Bruno didn't say anything, his father spoke up.

'Bruno hasn't had a day's trouble in his life, an' he's not used to these sort o' proceedin's. So if you don't mind, I'll just have my say an' get it over with.'

Vane looked towards Ruben who shrugged before nodding his agreement.

This time, Datch was more confident. 'I've already said, I was goin' to see my boy Bruno before he turned in. I wanted to see how he was settlin' in at bein' a deputy, figurin' he might be broodin' at havin' to kill a man. I heard the first shot and by the time I got to the jailhouse, Bruno was already bringin' Copper in. He told me what happened, that he'd seen Copper runnin' after and shootin' Silas Layborne.'

Ruben pushed himself away from the wall and raised his hand. 'For chris'sake, that's yet to be proved. It's not what we're here for.'

'Yeah, it's disallowed . . . inadmissible,' Vane said. 'Confine yourself to what you know happened, Datch. Not what you've been told.'

'Bruno saw someone runnin' away from the yard, an' he found Layborne dead with a bullet in his back. That was what he brought Copper in for. It was *him* on the run. I saw he wasn't carryin' a piece, so I went out an' found it. It was a small .36 Colt an' had one bullet missin'. It's as plain as day, an' so's the goddamn motive.'

Owen Copper looked quickly to Ruben, but Ruben's attention was on Grace McSwane. From her expression, it was plain she knew what Colvin Datch's last remark meant, and to Ruben, a silent plea to get her out of the situation.

'If you think you've discovered a motive, Datch, I'm sure we'll all be appreciative of it,' Vane pushed, and his tone was definitely harder.

'Well, I don't know, Judge. It's only somethin' I heard.'

'I'll make this an exception. Cut the sarcasm and get on with it.'

'It started yesterday, when Copper

an' Layborne got to tearin' into each other. It was in one of Ballard's stockyard pens, an' just about everyone in this room knows about it.'

'That will be everyone except me.'

'Yeah, judge excepted. Well, Layborne opened Copper's face. He beat him up bad, made a fool of him in front of those watchin'.'

Owen Copper jumped to his feet in angry protest, but Ruben moved in and pushed him back down, holding him there while he quietly said something. Copper ground his jaw, stared at Colvin Datch who grinned and continued with his assumed motive.

'Most men here will know that the boy's a troublemaker. Some would say no more'n a mouthy youngster . . . a braggadocio, especially where women are concerned. But they're the ones who cause trouble, an' this time it was over our new schoolteacher, Miss McSwane.'

Ruben cursed silently, let his eyes again drift towards Grace. As did most everyone in the room, even as Datch continued.

'It seems Layborne was mad at Copper for his lickerish claims about him an' the lady. *That* was what the fight was about. Copper wanted revenge, an' later he killed for it. Anybody says different needs proof to the contrary.'

8

Colvin Datch got to his feet and Bruno moved aside to let him pass. Ruben intervened before Datch was halfway back to his chair.

'What the hell's going on?' he demanded. 'There's a few questions I've got for him yet.'

Datch's shoulders heaved with emotion. 'I said my piece,' he replied tersely.

'As for your little outburst about anybody saying or thinking different, Mr Datch, I don't think you have much of a handle on the way our law works. Re-take your seat,' Billy Vane rasped with annoyance.

The room's silence deepened with anticipation as Colvin Datch walked slowly back towards Vane. The man brushed truculently at his suit, sat down stiffly and looked directly at Ruben. Defiance further pinched his sharp features.

'So, you actually witnessed the fight between Owen Copper and Silas Layborne?' Ruben put to him.

Datch frowned and shook his head. 'I was in the saloon watchin' Rites Noble shoot down our sheriff. Since Kayte's watchman was otherwise engaged, I let my boy handle the affair.'

'I'll take that as a straight no then. Tell me, how are you so sure, can even state categorically, that Layborne 'beat him up bad, and made a fool of him'? Tell us all, Mr Datch.'

'Hell, take a good look at him.'

Ruben nodded. 'I have. I was there. It was me who allowed the fight to go on. I considered the matter to be no more than jealousy, and they should lift the lid on any head of steam. I'm sure others who saw the fight will agree that neither man was hurt bad.'

'I'm sure they'll agree with anythin' you want 'em to,' Datch mumbled.

Ruben smiled tolerantly, lifted his hand to stop any rebuke. 'The motive put forward will hardly warrant a murder charge,' he continued. 'Maybe Mr Datch has personal reasons for exaggerating the spat, because a spat's all it amounted to.'

Datch clenched his fists. 'Goddamn you, Ballard. Are you callin' me a liar?'

'No, Mr Datch. I'm saying you're making allegations with little or no foundation, and I'm wondering why. Do we believe Owen Copper shot dead a deputy sheriff over a shiner and a fat lip? This is still a frontier town, not a goddamn nunnery.'

All colour drained from Datch's face. Bruno coughed and hunched his shoulders.

'You're not allowed to talk to my pa . . . Mr Datch like that,' he shouted.

'I am, and so is anybody else who has a point,' Ruben answered back quickly. 'So sit there peaceably while I call another man who can help with supporting evidence.'

'Relative, Mr Ballard?' Vane asked.

'I think so. Yes.'

'Call him up.'

Ruben spoke to a young man who was standing with an equally young woman on the other side of the bar room. 'No need to swear you in, Emilio. Just move in closer and answer my questions,' he called out.

Emilio Torres nodded. He looked at the woman beside him who smiled earnestly as they took a few steps closer to Ruben.

'Have you ever had an argument with Owen Copper?' Ruben asked.

'Sure,' Torres agreed immediately. 'We beat the beans out of each other.'

'For what, Mr Torres? What was the quarrel?'

'Mostly Angel.'

'Angel's your wife, isn't she?'

'Yes, she sure is.'

'Was this before or after you got married?'

'Before. Hell, everyone knows that, Mr Ballard.'

'We'd like to establish that from you, Mr Torres,' Billy Vane informed the young farmer. 'Please give straight questions a straight answer.'

'Can you tell us about this fighting?' Ruben requested.

'Owen would say Angel was sweeter on him than she was on me. I figured we ought to get it sorted. Me an' Angel were set to marry.'

'And you *did* get it sorted?'

'Sure. Took a few rounds, though.'

There was an instant clamour of amusement throughout the room, but it brought no response from Billy Vane.

'And there was no lasting ill feeling between the pair of you?' Ruben asked.

'No, sir. Even my jaw forgot it pretty quick. I certainly wouldn't expect him to shoot me in the back, like this rowdy dowdy show's tryin' to make out.'

Colvin Datch jumped to his feet. 'You stop *me*, but you're lettin' *him* sway people's minds with his hay-shaker opinion,' he rasped.

'A little tit for tat's not doing any harm,' Billy Vane returned. 'But be careful, Mr Ballard. I suppose there's a point here.'

'There certainly is. I'm saying there's two occasions when Owen Copper has been involved in a fracas over a woman. And they're probably not the first or last, either. But to allege he's come out a killer on the backs of them is downright ludicrous.'

'Hmm, point taken,' Vane said.

Again, Datch was on his feet and snarling. 'Ballard's jus' tryin' to muddy the water.'

There was growing unrest now throughout the provisional courtroom. Ruben tried to get the sense of the crowd, but Vane's banging soon ended the noise, and he was no nearer to knowing if his line of reasoning had been well taken.

'That's all, Mr Torres,' Vane decided, and turned to Ruben. 'Have you anything or anybody else, Mr Ballard?'

'Yes, there is one thing,' Ruben said, and the room returned to quiet again. 'I'm wondering how it's possible to know that the gun found out back of the jailhouse by Colvin Datch was the one that killed Silas. There's no proof. No one actually witnessed the shooting. As for the missing bullet, I know men who *always* carry an empty chamber under the hammer of their Colts. It's been known to save them shooting their toes off.'

'So, Mr Ballard?'

'So, without a shred of real evidence, this so-called hearing is nothing more than chop logic, an exercise in time wasting. Now, *and* in court. The only worthwhile achievement would be to uncover the *real* killer of Silas Layborne. It certainly wasn't Owen Copper.'

'I'll go with the time wasting,' Vane accepted. 'However, we do have a motive, a weapon *and* a suspect. Men have been hung for a lot less.'

Colvin Datch got to his feet and stared about the room. 'Yeah, Ballard's real touchin'. But Owen Copper works for him. He's bound to do what he can for the boy. Goin' with what the judge says, if all that legal stuff *sounds* helpful, it probably is. It's goddamn obvious.' Datch was beginning to sweat, and he ran a finger around the inside of his shirt collar.

Owen Copper looked at Ruben. 'What else we got to say, boss?'

Ruben nodded grimly. 'We've put it all out there, Owen. Now, it's a question of what others think.'

Colvin Datch looked smugly at Billy Vane. 'In the interest o' that time wastin', Judge, why not take your confederates out now? Like Ballard says, there's nothin' more on offer.'

Vane didn't waste any time on considering Datch's proposal. He rose and turned immediately towards one of the saloon's two private back rooms. A handful of men followed him, leaving the saloon proper to the rest of the gathering. Felix Shelter hardly had time to consider the chance of selling a few drinks, before Vane led the way back.

'Stand up, Copper,' he directed. 'In view of what's been heard here this morning, you'll continue to be held here for three days. The mail coach will transport you to Fort Yuma where you'll stand trial and get sentenced. That's it. Thank you all for attending.'

Vane picked up his weighty volume, without a backward glance, made his way from the saloon.

'Why'd you do it, Datch? Why me?' Copper snapped, a long moment later.

'I just gave evidence the way I saw it. You killed a man an' you got to pay for it. Plain an' simple.'

Bruno Datch nudged Copper in the back with his gun, who walked towards the swing doors, until he stopped in front of Grace McSwane. 'It was Silas all along, eh, miss?' he said.

Grace shook her head. She appeared to be tearful, unsure of how to respond. 'It wasn't any of you. You had no right to think otherwise. No right.'

Copper gave her a rueful smile. 'I know an' I'm sorry. But me an' Silas would've locked horns anyway, sooner or later. I guess we just used you for an excuse. But I never killed him.'

Bruno Datch held back, discomfited and not sure how to proceed. But without further prompting, Copper lifted his chin and walked from the saloon.

With his mind racing, Ruben stood for a long time, just staring out through the doorway, somewhere in the middle distance.

'You did your best, Ruben. Did what you could for Owen and for me,' Grace McSwane said, stepping up beside him. 'And I'm so grateful . . . indebted you didn't involve me any further. I know you could have.'

'You weren't involved, Grace. Not even in the beginning.' Ruben was going to try and explain further, but he caught sight of Tom Yurling and quickly gave his apologies.

'Rube. They're coming . . . only minutes behind,' Yurling blustered. 'It's Marley an' Rollo, an' they want to see you.'

Ruben nodded. 'I hope you told them it wasn't me. Tell them I'll be at the yard.'

Ruben wasn't sure he'd done everything he could, thought his lack of public address might be to blame. He heard a shout, the clink of Felix Shelter's whiskey glasses from the saloon behind him and realized how much he could do with a stiff drink. Stepping down from the boardwalk, he cursed as he crossed the street.

He couldn't accept that Owen Copper was capable of a murder, and certain that Colvin Datch had got the gain on him. But at the same time, he knew there wasn't any other decision the hearing assembly might have come to without being openly partisan. He crossed the yard and walked directly to his office. He snatched at a blanket, slumping deep in his tub chair to await the Copper brothers.

9

An hour later, they came together. Marley stomped his way through the doorway first. Rollo followed close, eagerly looking for Ruben.

'Mr Ballard, we've asked about, an' no one's told us there's somethin' to hold against you,' Marley Copper started without preamble. 'You did what you could, they say, an' did it good.' The man pulled a bench stool towards him, and Rollo Copper remained standing. 'An' we've spoken to Owen. We asked him right out; did he do it. Said it wouldn't matter much if he had. Said it, but didn't mean it. We just wanted the goddamn truth. He said he didn't, an' that's it.'

'He wouldn't lie to us, Mr Ballard,' Rollo said. 'Last time he did, he was about three. Ha, it didn't ever happen again.'

'No, not while we're eyeballin' each other, an' we just were,' Marley agreed. 'Nah, he didn't kill Silas Layborne.'

Ruben eased forward in his chair. 'Unfortunately, there's evidence he did, and Billy Vane made the only response he could. So hold nothing against *him*, either.'

Marley's lip curled with a thinly suppressed rage. 'You reckon we should just accept him givin' the nod for our brother's hangin'?'

Ruben knew the Coppers had already decided to fight for Owen's innocence. They would do it any way they could, and regardless of any due process or personal risk.

'It was a tad more than a nod, boys. He had no choice,' Ruben stressed. 'I couldn't convince him of Owen's innocence. If Vane failed him, it was because *I* failed him.'

Marley slammed a bunched fist into the palm of his hand, and Rollo spoke up again.

'Sometime back we talked about you,

Mr Ballard. Owen told us you were hard on him, kept him in line. We told him he needed someone, 'cause he wasn't a natural born sodbuster. He liked his liquor an' women too much. He was lost out there with only dust an' silence. We figured if he was to stay in town, it might as well be with you watchin' him, an' we were obliged.'

Ruben moved uneasily, trying to estimate what was coming.

'So, what do you think's happenin' here?' Marley asked. 'An' don't pussyfoot with the answer.'

'The happening already has. Inferred or not, the facts point to Owen being as guilty as hell. I thought I knew him well enough to doubt he'd shoot a man over a woman. Not in the back, anyway. But who's to know what happens between two armed men when they're breathing fire?'

'I know he didn't kill that deputy,' Marley snapped sourly. 'Let's not mull over why he could've.'

'You asked for a hardnosed answer.

That's it. If you don't like it . . . '

Marley took a short, angry breath. He kicked his stool away, and Rollo was quickly beside him.

'Well, the long game might not happen,' Marley said. 'Me an' Rollo are stayin' in town until we find the dung pile that shot Layborne. I've known an' respected you for a time, Mr Ballard. But in this, you're either with us or not. There's no middle way.'

Ruben stood up. He let the Navajo blanket wrap itself around the sawn off shotgun, laid it gently back on the seat of the tub chair.

The brothers took notice, looked quickly at each other in anxious surprise.

'Sometimes you need an edge,' Ruben answered their unspoken question. 'This could well have been the time. Thankfully for you, it wasn't.'

Marley Copper's face clouded a little. Again he looked at his brother, their eyes showing a deep message travelling between them.

'I know it must be hard to face this,' Ruben continued. 'I know you're a close family, but that can't affect what the hearing decides, and I have to go along with that. I have to. So, I won't help you, but if you find something . . . anything, let me know.'

Rollo nodded curtly, but again it was Marley who spoke.

'If Owen's on board that mail coach in three days' time, let's hope everyone stays clear o' the Yuma road.'

Ruben went to the door when Marley and Rollo had gone. He watched them walk towards the Shelter.

The saloon was fully open now, and Felix Shelter was standing by the swing doors, watching the street activity. He saw the Copper brothers headed his way and quickly turned back inside the building.

Ruben knew his loyalties were going to be divided. Owen Copper worked for him, but he couldn't let it be an influence. He locked the door of his office, walked across the yard and out through the main gate.

'We closin' up, Rube?' Tom Yurling, who had been watching and waiting, asked.

'Yeah, just for business. Tell the boys it's a water an' feed day.'

'I reckon they'd already guessed as much. I'll join you,' Yurling said, nodding in the direction of the Shelter.

Ruben asked for a bottle of good whiskey and went to sit at one of the card tables. He could see into the street which was now heating up, getting bright under the high sun. He didn't speak, and Yurling didn't interrupt him.

'I like working with horses, Tom. I really do,' he said eventually, his voice larded with feeling. 'They give the sort of trouble I'll take all day long.'

10

Colvin Datch came into the saloon at noon. From just inside the doorway he took a searching look at the bar counter, the drinking customers. There was a ripple of unrest hanging around, men making comments, passing an opinion on the morning's event. Some weren't in the saloon, didn't know Owen Copper all that well, but were nonetheless worried about the consequences of the hearing.

Datch sniffed determinedly and walked to Ruben's table. Ruben looked up but didn't offer acknowledgement.

'What do you want, Datch?' Tom Yurling asked.

'Horses.'

Ruben frowned, hardly looking up. 'What horses?' he replied. Out of the corner of his eye he saw Marley Copper push his brother back against the bar counter.

'I want a fresh team standin' by for the Yuma coach. I don't want any crow bait substitutes liable to break down halfway there. I don't trust any o' you sumbitches to play straight.'

'Well, this sumbitch don't stock crow baits. There's no real market,' Ruben tossed back. 'But why *you*, goddamn it? What the hell's it to you, Datch? What the hell is wrong with that boy of yours? You don't seem to trust him to carry out anything that needs more than a moment's thought.'

'I got Bruno elected to deputy because that's the work he said he wanted. But he's still got to be eased in. I don't know why you're so against him. He took Noble in a blink, didn't he? An' then he arrested a man an' got him charged with killin' Deputy Layborne. We got all that cleared in the hearin'.'

'You want to take charge of the horse team, there's a swing station fifteen miles out of town,' Ruben answered jadedly. 'See it gets done there.'

'You haven't taken to losin' out, have you, mister?' Datch pushed. 'Maybe it's the first time to anythin' or anybody in this town. Just make sure there's a team fresh an' ready for the Yuma run.'

'No need. They'll only be haulin' mail. Our brother won't be aboard,' Marley Copper joined in from across the room.

Datch whirled to face him, his face reddening with pressure. 'The town says he will,' he rasped. 'An' no one better try an' stop it, unless they want to clash with the new law.'

'Ah, go to hell, Datch. Nothin' about your Bruno amounts to a hill o' beans. But *you* do. There's been a lot o' talk about how you worked yourself into a sweat, gettin' Owen set up for trial. Some say if it wasn't for *you*, he'd still be playin' happy families.'

Datch stood his ground. He could feel the hostility emanating from those who knew Owen Copper, whether they were on friendly terms or not. 'The evidence was *against* your brother 'cause he shot a man in cold blood,' he replied. 'There's no point in gettin' in a stew about it. Remember it was him who pulled the goddamn trigger, not me.'

Marley Copper took a few steps towards Datch. 'My brother told me he didn't kill Silas Layborne. He looked me in the eye an' said it. An' that's somethin' *you'll* never understand, Datch.'

Ruben stood, but Rollo Copper was quick to intervene. 'Stay out of it, Mr Ballard,' he warned. 'This is about Marley not takin' to Owen bein' branded a liar. It's not your business.'

Ruben was grinding his teeth in aggravation, when Bruno Datch pushed through the swing doors. He knew immediately it wasn't coincidence, more like Bruno had been outside all along, listening.

Colvin Datch had known Marley and Rollo Copper were in the saloon, that they would intimidate him, or worse. His request for horses was timed. It was an expedient tactic, and the proof was evident across his face.

'You goin' up against the law o' this town, Copper? The law of the town, the county an' the State, goddamn it?'

Anxiety cut Marley Copper's face when he too realized they were being drawn. 'My brother don't hang. That's all,' he asserted with a quick glance towards Bruno Datch.

Ruben cut in quickly across the room. 'This isn't going to work. It won't happen,' he told Colvin Datch. 'There's proof your boy is very fast with a Colt. We don't want you crowding somebody else into getting killed. Why don't you get the hell out of here?'

Datch took a step backward. 'Mister, I keep tellin' you, you ain't runnin' this town. There's no safe hidin' behind Jefferson Kayte's friendship any more. Me an' Bruno wouldn't have moved aside for you then, an' we won't now.'

'You an' Bruno?' Ruben echoed incredulously. 'Who the hell's you an' Bruno? I don't recall you being voted

103

into any sort of Bonachon office.'

'It looks to me like the town's gone vinegary on him 'cause he did his duty. There could be some who's lookin' for a fight over what happened at the hearin' an' I'm not givin' 'em an edge. Even in this town, a deputy gets a backdoor man when he's on his rounds. So you keep it buttoned, Ballard. If I call their brother a liar, it stays that way until otherwise.'

Ruben's face clouded a little, and then angered when he saw Bruno take a step towards the Copper brothers.

Marley faced the newly appointed lawman, closely eyed the star of authority. Rollo Copper moved sideways, cursed before speaking.

'They ain't here to listen, Marl. We might as well take 'em.'

'Move a hand to your gun, an' I get to kill you. Just like I did Noble,' Bruno Datch said. 'I can do that easy. Pa's only doin' what people here told him was OK. So you leave him be.'

Marley Copper drew the back of his

hand across his mouth. He checked on Rollo who, for a moment, Ruben thought would back down.

Rollo considered the situation as though waiting for something more. But he didn't argue, and the silence deepened.

Marley moved away from the counter. Ignoring Colvin Datch, he confronted Bruno. 'You pull that Colt whenever you feel like it, boy,' he said. 'But be real mindful o' your options. Before I hit the floor, your pa will have half his gut shot away by Rollo. You're good, but not that good. Go right ahead an' see.'

Ruben saw the doubt lift in Bruno's face, began to maybe understand something of the youngster's character; his schooling of a gun to argue with, making it the answer to any challenge which might happen his way.

He stood between Bruno and Marley.

'No, this isn't the way,' he started. 'The town's given its opinion. Getting killed for it won't help, Marley. You or

Rollo or Owen.'

'The law's been challenged, Ballard, an' right now, the law's Bruno Datch,' Colvin Datch snarled. 'If you don't accept it, let's do somethin'. Let's see who runs the town, you or Bruno.'

'Yeah, why not.' Marley nodded agreeably. 'We'll let the men here decide what happens, same way they decided this morning. They're more or less the same gather, if you'll pardon the term.'

Bruno looked puzzled, turning to his father for guidance. Datch was suddenly troubled at seeing the situation slipping from his control.

'I've said my piece, Ballard. If Bruno's to police this town, then he's got to prove himself. Those who've decided they don't want him, have got to know who an' what they're rejectin'.'

'I think they'll understand, just as I do. Bruno has to learn that his duty as duly elected lawman isn't to kill under your persuasion, but to stop trouble. There's a difference,' Ruben said. 'Now we'll see who wants this fight to happen. When it's done, Datch, you get out of here and teach your boy the community style of Jeff Kayte. Difficult for you I can imagine, but not impossible. If you don't, I'll call another goddamn meeting, have the hearing annulled and stand against Bruno myself. If your worst fears are right, you know who'll win that one.'

Felix Shelter, quick to back Ruben, called out from the bar. 'You all heard that. Those against another gunfight, hold your hands up.'

Ruben kept his attention fixed on Colvin Datch while just about every hand in the room was lifted. One or two men enthusiastically lifted both. Marley Copper cursed when his own brother's hand went up, when he saw him mouthing, 'just saved your life'.

'Looks like a vote against, then,' Ruben confirmed. 'Let that be a first lesson, Bruno. If you want to work for the interests of Bonachon, you've got to learn from its people . . . us, and not be swayed by the wind your father blows.'

Showing a mix of disappointment and worry, Bruno Datch stared back sourly at Ruben. The gunfight had been stopped, and it was clear he didn't know which move to make from there on.

Colvin Datch was numbed from the shock of being openly defeated. 'OK, Ballard, you got the vote you wanted, an' my boy will stand by it,' he said. 'But the Coppers best remember, as far as Bruno's concerned, he's keepin' watch on someone who's goin' to be tried for murder. When the time comes he's proved himself, you can stand against him then, if the mood still takes you.'

Datch motioned for Bruno to move out ahead of him. After a mean glance at Marley and Rollo Copper, he followed on into the street.

Ruben cursed under his breath, gave an indication for Shelter to replace his whiskey bottle.

'There's somethin' wrong about all

this, Rube,' Tom Yurling muttered. 'An' I'm thinkin' the sooner it's settled, one way or another, the better for every-body.'

'Yeah, I know. I wish Jeff was here so's I could ask him what to do.' Ruben poured himself a very large measure of liquor and swallowed it in one deter-mined gulp. 'I'll sort out the big buckskin for Jake Tedstone,' he said. 'For the next couple of days, we'd better keep the boys in work, Tom. We don't want them getting in a state about Owen, else we'll have an uprising to deal with.'

Ten minutes later, Ruben was near-ing the end of town. He was crossing to his stockyard when he saw Colvin Datch emerge from the boarding house. It wasn't so much the presence of Datch, as that of a smiling Grace McSwane that interested, then both-ered him.

Sitting behind his desk, estimating on the Tedstone account, he couldn't get the image of Grace McSwane and

Colvin Datch from his mind. He pulled open a side drawer and lifted out a slim, leather bound notebook. It was a gift from his grandparents after he told them he was going into business. They had penned inside the front cover, *If it's business, write down their names, and trust none of them.*

'What sort of business?' he muttered, uncorking a bottle of Wild Turkey. As Tom Yurling also suspected, Ruben knew Datch was up to something, but he also knew that his own suspicions were slight and ill-founded. He took a single pull of the whiskey, placed the bottle on the desk in front of him. Considering the situation more sideways on, Bruno had risked his life against the gunsman, Rites Noble. And, as Owen Copper acknowledged, he had followed up the shot out back of the jailhouse by coming directly to check it out. Maybe the act of a budding lawman, Ruben thought. Maybe.

Ruben placed his notebook back in the drawer and got to his feet. He paced

110

around the office, getting more confused as he thought about Bruno Datch's behaviour.

Since the hearing, Bruno hadn't put a foot wrong, let alone a bullet. He even gave his testimony calmly and without hostility. So, was it Colvin Datch who was the problem? Actually, he'd done nothing but urge his son into a responsible position, wanting to give him support until he was settled. What was so wrong with that?

'I know something's not right. Needs a better brain than mine to figure it, though,' Ruben muttered. He went out into the afternoon's heat, tugged at the brim of his range hat and headed across to the boarding house.

11

Jake Tedstone snorted angrily as he squinted through a side window of his ranch house. He adjusted his gunbelt and grabbing a rifle, he stomped from the house.

Two riders were at a steady gallop, bearing down on him after crossing his home pasture. The men rode steady, their features and clothing were stark and they both had carbines resting behind saddle horns. Some distance behind the two riders, another two men were running the select herd of Herefords.

Earlier in the day, Tedstone had discovered the cows were missing from his lower range. He'd followed them to the western end of his land, then he'd picked up the sound of their restless movement across the vast silence. He rarely carried a gun on his morning check but, sensing trouble, he rode fast back to his ranch house to get one.

Now, on the steps down from his veranda and into the sun, he stopped, looked up and levered a bullet into the chamber of his Winchester. Take more'n a greasy sack outfit to run off my cattle, he was thinking.

A sudden gust of wind whipped up high and caught him full in the face. For a moment he was blinded by acrid dust and he spat and cursed. He lifted the barrel of his rifle, threatening as the riders closed in.

When the two men were through the logged yard entrance, they spread apart until there was thirty feet or more between them. The rider on the left fired first, his shot ripping into Tedstone's left shoulder.

Tedstone reeled back against a veranda pillar as a second bullet hit him in the thigh. He felt no pain, just thwarted anger when he dropped his rifle. He pulled his Colt, held himself steady as he fired in retaliation.

A young rider gasped, held his rifle up above his head, before slipping sideways and down from the saddle.

'You want them cows, you goddamn pay for 'em,' Tedstone yelled hoarsely at the body sprawled in the dust. He collapsed to one knee, looked at the ground and saw he was kneeling in a pool of his own blood. 'It's taken me years to create this little herd,' he muttered quietly.

The second rider, who wore a slouch hat and bleached duster, looked to his fallen companion and swerved his mount away. He came at Tedstone from the right, for a second, bringing his horse between himself and the wounded stock breeder.

Tedstone now clenched his teeth against the surge of pain. Another bullet sliced across his forehead, and he felt as though he'd been struck by a hammer. He sunk to the hard-packed dirt of his yard, unbelieving that his own dust could fill his mouth and eyes, a thick warm carpet that was suffocating him.

He pushed his head from the ground, looking up at nothing but a blurred mix of light and dark. Then he heard the thud of hooves, the snap and creak of leather as the horse was being dragged to a halt nearby.

'Why the hell didn't you stay inside?' the raspy voice exclaimed. 'We'd have passed by.'

Tedstone tried to swallow, lick his lips. He lifted himself a fraction, suddenly pleased that he'd sent his girls over to spend a couple of days with George Stillman's kids. Have to spend the rest o' their lives without my guidance, he thought. Perhaps the school ma'am can take 'em under her wing. No reason to come home weekends, either.

'Because they're mine, an' you're not takin' 'em,' he choked out.

'We already did, mister. Go back to sleep.' With that, the rider put a final bullet into Tedstone's body.

That'll do it, Tedstone thought, feeling the thud of impact, the incredible crush on his life. An' how the hell was I supposed to know she was ill? His mind started to wander. Why didn't she tell me? These were thoughts of his wife, long since dead. Then it was Jeff Kayte. Him bein' taken like that . . . hopeless boy deputy. It felt like an immense muscular hand had reached inside him, dragging him somewhere he didn't want to go. Why can't I see the son of a bitch? He wondered about the second armed rider. Where is he? I could shoot him.

A light wind stroked Tedstone's face, turning it cold. He tried to spit the dust away, but there was no fight left. He felt blood oozing across his eyelids, then the chill again, then nothing.

★　★　★

Grace McSwane was sitting in the shaded north corner of the boarding house's foyer. She was reading an old Tucson broadsheet, appearing relaxed, well at ease. She looked up and smiled, before quickly frowning at Ruben

Ballard's stern countenance.

'I saw Colvin Datch here earlier. What were you talking about?' Ruben started off without preamble.

Grace shook her head slightly, as if making a correction to what she heard. 'Sorry, Ruben,' she said. 'What on earth's it to do with you? Gracious, this town's obsessed about who I'm seen talking to.'

'If you knew anything about the man, you'd understand why I want to know,' he replied. 'Have you forgot what happened at that so-called hearing? The way he played for the hanging of young Owen Copper?'

'You know I haven't forgot, Ruben. But I don't see how that gives you the right to question me.'

'Perhaps it doesn't, but you said you wanted to be accepted . . . to further yourself in Bonachon. Well, chumming with the likes of Colvin Datch isn't going to help. Believe me, that's another thing you'll have to rectify.'

Grace stood up, flushing and a little

angrier. 'I don't *chum* with anyone, Mr Ballard. Have you taken the role of counsellor, now?'

Ruben was taken aback by the quick response. He hadn't known how Grace would respond to his question, but he felt obligated because he'd already wronged her over Owen Copper and Silas Layborne. He was telling himself this could be a way towards putting things right.

'No, and it looks like maybe I've butted in somewhere I shouldn't,' he replied, drawing back a pace. 'I didn't realize . . . didn't think. I'm sorry.' He turned to leave but Grace spoke up again.

'Don't go, Ruben. I didn't say I wanted that.'

He glanced back, held her gaze for a moment. There was a trace of a smile, but still some reserve.

'It was none of my business. I got it wrong . . . shouldn't have happened.'

'Well, perhaps you didn't get it *all* wrong. I'm sure you have your reasons.

I know you're a man the townspeople respect. I'm the one who's a stranger, and have no wish to incur your disapproval.'

'I don't disapprove of you, Grace. Exactly the opposite,' he said, faltering. He didn't know how to handle the situation he'd created, but wasn't in charge of.

'I'll tell you why Mr Datch visited me, why he was here,' Grace continued. 'To make me a proposition. A *business* proposition. It's nothing personal, if that's what still concerns you, Ruben.'

'Business? What business? I thought you were a schoolteacher.'

'Yes, I am, and I must admit, Mr Datch did disturb me by his approach. But I'll tell you what happened next if you'll listen.'

Ruben nodded, indicated that Grace sit down again. He put his hat under his arm and perched on the end of an adjacent sofa.

'He must have been prepared, because what he said came out quick enough,' Grace continued. 'He said he wasn't much regarded in Bonachon, and didn't blame anyone but himself. He wanted to do better, get some standing.'

Ruben gave a wry smile and Grace returned it. 'Yes, it did remind me of someone,' she agreed. 'He insisted that none of it was for him. It was all for the sake of his son, Bruno. He knew that some people — and you were one of them — thought Bruno was a bad 'un, because of his own past wrongdoings.'

Ruben shook his head with incredulity and Grace went on quickly.

'I know, but please don't make premature judgements again, Ruben. I wasn't impressed or influenced by his speechifying, but I did think he meant what he was saying . . . what he was offering.'

'Yeah, and what was that?' Ruben asked indifferently.

'Two hundred dollars towards the building of a new schoolhouse and annex.'

'What? What's that got to do with his son?'

'It would be him, Bruno, recorded as the donor. It wouldn't be the first time that's happened with benefactors, I'm sure. Like a sleeping partner in business. What's wrong with that?'

Ruben turned and looked into the parlour. A group of men were sitting at a table drinking coffee, but didn't appear to be interested in himself or Grace McSwane.

'Nothing. It does happen, for all sorts of reasons,' he said. 'But to my knowledge, Colvin Datch has never had more than *two* dollars in his pocket, let alone *two hundred*. Not that actually belonged to him, anyways. When does this big-heartedness get real?'

'About a week. When he's got one or two matters settled.'

'When he's robbed one or two banks, more like.'

Grace stood up and looked stern. 'I need the money, Ruben. I need every dollar I can get. I'm eager to get the school up and running.'

To reply on equal terms, Ruben also got to his feet. 'There's plenty of other folk, willing to help, Grace,' he advised. 'You really don't have to get mixed up with Colvin Datch. Look, I came here with something on my mind, I might as well tell it.'

Grace gave a slight nod, and Ruben continued his explanation.

'Bonachon's a small town and most of its people *think* small. For all sorts of reasons, Datch has never been invited in. So increasing his standing here is something I can understand. But believe me, Grace, you have that name on your sponsor list and what you want to happen, won't. The buildings might, but there'll be no kids inside, and your status will just fade away. There, I've said what I came here to. You can make up your own mind.'

Ruben turned away. He had taken a couple of paces towards the front door, when Grace put her hand around his forearm. She was closer to him than they had been sitting on the rig seat. The group of men in the parlour now looked up, one of them saying something quietly to the other two.

Ruben shook his head sadly. 'You were right,' he said. 'It's nothing to do with me. I should have minded my own business. I'll try to in future. Good day, ma'am.'

★　★　★

Ruben started work again on his bottle of Wild Turkey. He was angry because he realized how it must look to Grace; making a mutt of himself in his persistent, near boorish problem with Colvin Datch,

He poured another fat measure, decided the Datches could momentarily go to blazes. He was thinking about his contract for Jake Tedstone, when Tom Yurling came in. He didn't look up, waited for Yurling to say something.

'Our Miss McSwane got under your hide, has she?' his foreman said.

Ruben pondered on his words for a moment. 'Yeah, she's obviously got the gift.'

Yurling grinned easily. 'Perhaps you're makin' it easy for her.'

Ruben looked harder at him. He took on the grin, reading enough to see there was nothing untoward or critical. 'Don't go getting any ideas,' he said.

Yurling moved to the coffee pot. Feeling it wasn't even warm, he put some kindling into the stove.

'I'm not,' he replied. 'But just in case you were, Rube, I'd be a tad careful. Look what happened to Silas an' Owen.'

'Yeah, I did notice.' Ruben went and stood in the doorway, stared across the yard through the gate to the town's main street. He knew the structure and being of the town as well as his own stockyard. But right now, he didn't. It was as if a lifeblood had drained away. He knew not all, but the best part of the trouble was created by the presence of Colvin Datch and his son who was legally posted in the jailhouse.

'Colvin Datch has offered two hundred dollars towards building the schoolhouse,' he said tersely.

'Two hundred dollars? Huh, how the hell's *he* got that sort o' money?'

'That's more or less what I thought . . . what I said. It's obviously a poke to get him the status he says he wants.'

'She didn't accept it, did she?' Yurling asked quickly.

'I reckon she will. She wants to get something going.'

Yurling shook his head doubtfully, for emphasis, moved away from the stove, closer to Ruben. 'Well, if she uses it, she'll be makin' a mistake. Hell, Ruben, you're the only one I know who's got that sort o' dough by doin' somethin' legal.'

Ruben gave a wry smile in return, and Yurling realized the cause of the man's prickly disposition.

'Is that what's brought on this brown study?' he pushed.

'More likely, her telling me it's her

business, that she's her own woman.'

Yurling was silent for a moment. 'An' you'd really like her to be yours,' he suggested. 'Do you think that's it?'

'If it was, I wasn't going to tell her.'

'Well, going back to the Datch thing. I can't think of many who'll sign up to any committee with the Datch name on it. Whether his son's a lawman or not. I can usually smell a storm on the way, Rube. This one could bring the geese down.'

'Yeah,' Ruben agreed. 'And there's nothing we can do about it. We'll pack Owen off to Fort Yuma to get sentenced and hung. There'll be indignant sickness for a while, and with no shortage of encouragement, Marley and Rollo will fight anyone. Grace McSwane will get her bastion of learning built because she's that sort of woman, and Jake Tedstone will have his new stables and an even better line of Herefords. All business back to normal. But it won't ever be the same, Tom. The town slipped its tether when

126

Jeff Kayte got himself killed.'

'Have you got an answer to it?' Yurling asked.

'I'll get me that tent I told you about, and move further west. Perhaps I won't stop until I reach the Pacific. They're growing oranges and lemons out there, you know?'

Yurling looked at his long time friend and felt the dejection. He thought about the short homily, realizing that Ruben had never spoken to him before of anything similar. He was aware that something was shifting in the town, and now Ruben was too.

'Coffee's started to boil,' he said a moment later. 'At least this won't change. It'll be as bad as it ever was.' The two men sat in silence. There was little of the town's normal convivial sound drifting towards them.

12

It was an hour after sundown. The town remained unusually quiet, and Ruben Ballard was sitting on the stoop of his office. He saw Grace McSwane walk from the boarding house across the street towards the site of the proposed schoolhouse. She was accompanied by two of Bonachon's important ladies, those who organized community functions. Ruben was impressed by the way Grace was already making herself part of the town, someone meaning to stay around and leave a mark.

'Makes it a bit easier when folk are backing your ideas with bundles of cash,' he muttered to no one in particular.

'The boys are set for an early start tomorrow, Rube,' Tom Yurling called out. 'You want me to go along?'

Ruben looked up and shook his head.

'No. I'll feel better once I've cleared town. A couple of days with dumb wood's what I need.'

'Suit yourself. I'll put together what you'll need. How long will you be out there?'

'We'll get into the west timber, and take down some tall stuff. It's harder, but makes the building that much easier. Say three or four days . . . two or three nights.'

'OK. I'll leave you to your thoughts then,' Yurling said, and did for most of the rest of the day.

It was first dark when Yurling went to the saloon. He thought he'd be more comfortable there, seeing about tomorrow's ride out to the Tedstone ranch. And he could relax a bit, talk to Felix Shelter, to whom he'd hardly spoken since the shootings of Rites Noble and Jefferson Kayte.

As he crossed the hard, sandy main street, Yurling wondered if in fact it had been more than two days. It seemed like a month, with so much happening meantime. He went into the saloon and quickly sought out the Ballard hands. He advised them on the work to be packed and ready to ride at sunup the following morning. Then he settled an elbow on the bar, savoured his first beer of the evening.

Felix Shelter waited until his customers were well supplied, before he mentioned his doubts to Yurling.

'Don't you fret none about goin' against Rube. You know he never holds a grudge,' Yurling replied.

'Well, perhaps he will this time. I backed Colvin Datch to give Bruno a chance. That wasn't what Ruben wanted. Not by a long chalk.'

'That's as maybe, Felix, but it don't mean to say he's right. Perhaps Bruno should be given one. It's votin' for what you want. All the rage in some parts.'

'You don't believe that. You're just sayin' it.' Shelter swiped at the counter with a sodden rag, making an even broader and dirtier pool. 'Hell, Tom, you weren't here to see the boy take

130

Noble,' he went on. 'When you see that ability you just got to go with it. Specially if it's on your side.' Shelter shook his head as if still unable to believe what he'd witnessed. 'Fastest I ever saw, an' I'm goin' back a bit.'

'It's not Bruno Datch that me or Rube's particularly worried about, Felix. It's his pa,' Yurling said. 'He's pushin' too hard. You ever know a man so keen to have his boy killed?'

'Have you thought that Datch sees Bruno as so good, nobody's goin' to harm him? Have you thought that?'

'Hmmm.' Yurling was flummoxed. He stared at Shelter, who had turned to look at something happening at the other end of the room.

Marley Copper had got up from a card table. He was walking towards his brother, Rollo, who was already halfway to one of the saloon's rear doors.

Yurling recognized the elaborate gait of men who'd done a few hours serious drinking. He saw the drunken stare of Marley's eyes, the way he held his brother's attention.

'They've been here most o' the day,' Felix Shelter said. 'Hardly moved . . . just sat broodin'. Now my liquor's caught up with 'em.'

'I don't think so,' Yurling replied quietly. He stepped back from the counter, finished his drink in one and nodded a farewell. From the open back door, he saw the Coppers moving into the alleyway that ran behind the main street buildings. He followed them, holding back in the deep shadow, when they stopped at the end of the alley.

The pair turned left. It wasn't a place that Yurling frequented, and he tried to work out exactly where they were. In the near darkness, he passed a dilapidated pole corral and a low adobe building which he knew had been the town's first livery stable. He understood where they were then, and the consequence brought out a low curse.

The alley suddenly angled towards the jailhouse yard. A bleak quarter where nobody had any business unless it was to empty trash. Or get 'emselves shot, he thought grimly.

He cursed again and hurried back more or less the way he'd come. This time he ran past the saloon and continued on to the stockyard.

'That trouble . . . the goose downer I mentioned,' he came out with breathlessly. 'The first drops have just fell.'

'What do you mean?' Ruben Ballard asked.

'Why would the Coppers get loaded, then go skulkin' in an alley on the west side o' Main Street?'

Ruben considered the layout in his mind for a moment. 'They wouldn't. Nobody would, unless it was to break Owen out of the jailhouse,' he suggested.

Yurling nodded. 'Yeah. I'd wager on it.'

Ruben groaned and dropped his head in disappointment. 'They're headed for a lot more trouble than they can handle,' he muttered. 'Did you see if they were wearing guns?'

'Marley had what looked like an old Dragoon's Colt tucked in his belt. Don't know about Rollo.'

'Wait here, Tom.' Ruben got to his feet, and in one movement went straight past his foreman. Out of the yard he hesitated, looked up to see the twin oil lamps had been lit outside the jailhouse at the far end of the street.

Approaching the Shelter Saloon, Ruben recalled words he'd heard Jefferson Kayte use on more than one occasion. 'If you go looking for trouble, you'll surely find it,' the tough sheriff had reckoned. Ruben was speculating whether to some people, trouble was a maggot in the brain, an addiction, when the first gunshot broke the night's uneasy silence.

From the stockyard, Tom Yurling waited and watched. Then he followed on, cursing and breaking into a run as Ruben had done a second before him.

★　★　★

For the umpteenth time, Bruno Datch used his thumb to roll the cylinder of his Colt. 'But how do you know?' he asked his father.

'If it was *you* sittin' in that goddamn bull pen, an' you had two brothers, don't you think they'd be here? It's a question o' timin'. When the booze starts its work.'

'But when's *that*?'

Colvin Datch looked tolerantly at his son. 'Well, it's goin' to be *before* they get Copper's ass aboard the mail coach, that's for sure. It won't be long now, believe me, an' no more difficult than a regular beef kill. Just think, Bruno, if you settle this trouble, there ain't goin' to be man nor beast who don't fully appreciate your work. Fully accepted. A hawk an' a spit away from becomin' Bonachon's big augur.'

Bruno shoved his Colt back in his holster, pushed at his nose with the back of his hand. He wasn't particularly worried about more trouble. In his own callow way, he now regarded such situations as normal. But he was mindful of Ruben Ballard's hostility towards his father, his father's mutual stance. There was no problem in Bruno's mind as to loyalty, although he would have Ruben Ballard as a friend rather than an enemy.

'Looks like you were right, Pa,' he said after ten more minutes staring into the gloom. 'This'll be them.'

Colvin Datch was quick to his feet, standing behind Bruno at the back door of the jailhouse. He cursed excitedly, pushing Bruno down the steps into the darkness of the yard, crouching to the near side of the trash cans.

'What did you see?' he whispered.

'Somethin' moved in the shadows. Can't be rats that big out there.'

'We'll let 'em go for their brother, then nail 'em red-handed.'

Bruno screwed his face up with doubt. 'We let 'em inside?'

'Yeah, just like I said,' Datch insisted. 'Couple o' minutes more. When this is settled, I've got someone in mind to make one hell of a deputy . . . *your* deputy, Bruno. Together, we'll hog-tie Bonachon. Gettin' even's been a few years in the waitin', so don't question me now.'

Bruno nodded grimly. He had another look at his Colt and hunkered dutifully in the deep shadow between a bin and a big water barrel.

Marley and Rollo Copper came slowly along the alley from the back street. They were moving stiffly and cautiously, their eyes now fixed on the partly open rear door of the jailhouse. They stopped for a moment and Marley pulled a belly gun from his coat pocket and handed it to Rollo.

'Use it if you have to. Owen's our brother,' he rasped expressively.

'Door's open, Marl. Makes it easier,' Rollo replied as they approached the trash cans.

'Funny thing to do . . . considerin'.' There was suddenly a note of uncertainty in Marley's voice. 'Datch can't be that stupid. Can you see in there

. . . hear anythin'?'

'Nothin'. There's a light goin' though. You don't think they've gone, do you?'

'No. Where'd they go?'

The pair continued close to the rear door before Marley could see for himself into the jailhouse. When he saw nothing ahead, he edged up the steps, flattening himself against the inside wall. He motioned for Rollo and holding his gun before him, they stepped further into the building, looking straight towards the cells and the sheriff's office. The tension was driving out any lingering Dutch courage, and he grunted thickly at still hearing nothing.

'Goddamn it, Marl, it's too easy,' Rollo wheezed. 'Who the hell's in there? Shall I call for Owen?'

Marley shook his head, vigorously. 'Do things quiet until we know.'

'Do what?'

'Go in an' get the keys. They'll be close at hand, probably hangin' some-where. I'll be close behind, watchin' for you,' Marley replied.

Rollo hesitated and Marley nudged him forward. 'If they were here, we'd know by now, goddamn it. I'm worried about Owen, but don't say anythin'.'

The keys were lying on the desk, and Rollo quickly picked them up. He turned them in the lamp light, then looked nervously around as he crossed to his brother's cell.

'Rollo. What the hell's going on?' Owen called out the moment he set eyes on his brother. 'Where'd you come from?'

'The alley. Where's the Datches?'

'Dunno. They were here ten minutes ago. Didn't you see 'em?'

'No one got past us. I'll set you free an' we'll cut out quick. Marl's here.'

Owen Copper was breathing heavily, impatiently pushing on the bars until Rollo clicked open the lock. He ran straight out to where Marley was standing guard. For the first time in days, he grinned as he was shoved straight out through the door into the yard.

Marley was telling him to run for the alley. 'An' get yourself to the edge o' town,' he shouted, a moment before the first shot from Colvin Datch crashed out.

13

The bullet smashed into Owen Copper's chest. It stopped him dead, then he reeled, staggered halfway back into the jailhouse.

'There's two more. You can get 'em both,' Datch directed Bruno.

As Marley Copper stepped into the low light of the doorway, Bruno stepped from the shadows and his Colt flashed. But at the instant he fired, Marley dropped to tend his brother and Bruno's shot caught him high across the top of his shoulder. Target. Should've snuffed the lamp, he thought as he fell alongside Owen.

Even though he was half-expecting something to happen, Rollo was stunned by the outbreak of gunfire, but with both hands clasped around the Dragoon's Colt, he ran around his fallen brothers. He fired furiously into the darkness, hurling himself from the doorway and across the steps.

There was a shout from Colvin Datch, and Bruno started to run towards the jailhouse doorway.

Rollo was in the yard now. He veered to the left but before he could gain the relative darkness of the alleyway, Bruno Datch had caught sight of him, putting a bullet somewhere into his lower body. His old Colt misfired and he cursed, trying to run on. He pitched forward, nearly made it, but he tripped and fell, remaining very still after hitting the ground.

'You got 'im, Bruno. Now finish 'em off while I cover you,' Colvin Datch rasped. 'They're the sort who'll shoot you from the grave.'

Bruno heard his father and responded. From the steps, he looked down on Owen and Marley Copper. He pushed the door fully open, listened and stepped into the jailhouse.

He was about to have a closer look at the unmoving bodies when Ruben

Ballard suddenly appeared from the front office. Instinctively, his Colt was raised and the impulse to shoot knotted his features.

'Regular back-door trash,' Ruben snarled. 'Put that goddamn Colt down.'

Bruno glared for a moment, and then his father stepped up beside him and levelled his own gun on Ruben.

'An' that includes you, Datch,' Tom Yurling shouted. 'Your killin's done for tonight.'

Ruben half turned. 'I thought I said to wait at the yard,' he said.

'Yeah, you did,' Yurling agreed. 'What you goin' to do about it?'

Datch looked angrily at the two stockmen. 'You were in on this. The both o' you,' he charged.

Lowering his gun, Ruben walked towards Datch. He looked down at Owen Copper's lifeless body and cursed. 'If we had been in on anything, it would have been you two scum-suckers lying here,' he seethed in response.

'It was my boy who stopped 'em,' Colvin Datch snapped. 'They were breakin' that killer out an' Bruno took 'em. I helped. There's no room for you or your sway in this, Ballard.'

Ruben returned the older man's look of loathing. Then he leant down and looked closely at Marley Copper. He cursed again and, shoving his Colt away, lifted and propped him against the inner jailhouse wall.

Colvin Datch took a step closer. 'He's still alive?'

'Yeah. I guess your budding trigger man made a mistake.'

Colvin Datch took a steadying breath. 'We don't make that sort o' mistake, Ballard, an' you best remember it. We heard noises outside an' went to investigate. That's when those Copper boys must've snaked in. When we saw 'em next, Bruno shouted for 'em to halt. But they came out shootin', an' we had to take 'em down. To my way o' thinkin', it's called upholdin' the law. That one in the cell ran with 'em.'

Ruben considered what the older man had said. 'And I'm from Dixie Land,' he returned. 'You've always got your answer.'

Datch was angered again. 'I got answers, because I say what happens, Ballard. Not what's dreamt up. An' now I'm gettin' real sick o' you buckin' me an' my boy. So listen an' listen good. Bruno's got the right to prod anybody he likes, an' if he takes it into his head to figure you're a trouble-maker, then that's what you'll be, whether you got friends in this town or not.'

Ruben gave a cold, wry smile. 'I wouldn't have put speechifying down as one of your strong suits, Datch,' he said, and turned his attention to Bruno.

'How about you, Deputy? What's *your* bedtime story?' he asked.

'Same as Pa's. That's how it happened, an' like he says, we're too full o' your interferin'. I'm no range kid who don't know what he's at. So you get the hell away from here an' let me handle things.'

'You or your pa?' Ruben said sharply. When Bruno grunted out his anger, Ruben slowly turned his back on him. He indicated to Tom Yurling to help him pick up and carry Marley Copper.

Colvin Datch moved quickly. 'What the hell are you up to now, Ballard? Didn't you hear what Bruno . . . the deputy sheriff just said?'

'The man needs a doctor. We'll take him to one.'

'He's taken part in a goddamn jail-break. That's a felony against Bonachon, if ever there was one.'

'You're a piece of work, Datch, and I thank God you weren't my pa. The man's hurt bad and needs help, so he's getting it. Help him up, Tom.'

Yurling moved forward, but Colvin Datch hadn't finished.

'What happens later?' he wanted to know. 'He could have killed Bruno . . . an elected peace officer.'

'*Later*, he can maybe go to trial for *not* shooting *you* dead, Datch. That's an eighteen-carat felony against the

146

town, if ever there was one.'

Between them, Ruben and Yurling supported Marley Copper, walking him slowly and carefully to the front door of the jailhouse.

Ruben wasn't sure if Bruno would back his father for action, or if Colvin Datch would continue to argue. They were at the door when Datch had his last say.

'I'm makin' you responsible, Ballard,' he threatened. 'You want it, you got it. An' I'll let the whole goddamn town know.'

★   ★   ★

From the boardwalk, Ruben looked across the street to those who were drawn by the gunfire. They were shoulder to shoulder, excited and alarmed.

Without acknowledgment or explanation, Ruben led the way through them towards the Bonachon doctor's practice.

Louis Barker had been a field

surgeon during the War Between the States. Now he was near retirement, didn't rest easy any more. He had heard the gunfire, was already expecting customers in his surgery.

'Lucky it wasn't an inch or so to the left,' he said, after a brief examination. 'He wouldn't have had much of a throat left, be dead more'n likely. The way it is, he won't be wielding much for a few weeks. Leave him with me. I'll clean him up.'

Ruben thanked Barker. 'Charge it to the town. Say it's collateral damage,' he suggested.

Colvin Datch was standing outside the saloon. True to his word, he was running down Ruben to anyone who'd listen. It was where drunks occasionally disturbed the peace, shouted their troubles to indifferent passers-by.

'He don't miss an opportunity, does he?' Yurling said. 'If he keeps this prattle up, one or two folk might start to see Bruno as the real McCoy. Next thing, he'll be on the ticket with his boy as Governor.'

'Either that or one of those puppeteer music hall acts.'

Five minutes later, Ruben walked tiredly into his stockyard. Again, he was feeling at odds with the town and its people, his so-called friends. Men like Felix Shelter whom he'd seen listening to Datch's tirade and not in obvious disagreement.

He was back to thinking that a day and a night out of town would calm him down, let him experience an alternative existence. He was wondering what kind of fish were in Grapevine Creek when Grace McSwane tapped on his office door. Through the glass panel he saw she was looking less self-assured than the last time he'd seen her.

He opened the door and pushed a chair forward. 'You look like you need a sit down,' he said. 'What's up? It's a tad late for a social visit.'

'It's difficult to sleep through a fourth of July style celebration.'

'Oh that, yeah. We had ourselves

another shooting . . . shootings.' Ruben stopped short of telling of how Colvin Datch was involved.

Grace sat down, and looked around her. 'You know what they say about drinking on your own?' she asked.

'Some might suggest it's not as good as doing it with a temperate schoolma'am.'

'Well, you don't want to settle for second best, do you?'

Intrigued, Ruben poured a large Wild Turkey and handed her the glass. 'Only the best. Even though you didn't come here to drink or exchange improper banter,' he said with a wry smile.

'Thank you. I've been thinking again about Colvin Datch. What you tried to tell me.'

'Go on.'

'A group of townswomen I'm getting involved with have suggested that he might well be a lot closer to the person you were warning me off. I've been well advised to make sure of the provenance of any donation before it's accepted.'

'I thought something like that might

happen,' Ruben said. 'Some of those ladies are sharper than tacks.'

'Yes, so I've discovered. And fortunately, I'm still able to have the benefit of hindsight. But it wasn't just what you and the ladies said, Ruben. Giving money to a cause like this should be more considerate . . . sincere. Certainly to appear like it. But thinking about it now, it was a bit self-seeking, even if it wasn't for him personally. And then being asked to wait a while.'

'Yeah, very odd. Any of us could've offered that,' Ruben agreed, and feeling a little more amenable.

'He said something else that maybe I should mention.'

'What was that?'

'He said an influential businessman named Prior . . . Virgil Prior, was about to settle an account with him. It was a deal he'd been working on for a long time.'

'Did he say who this Virgil Prior actually was? More to the point, what he did?'

'No. Only that with such powerful backing, nobody in town could disregard him. Not even you. It was something like that.'

'Hmm. Damned with faint praise, eh? And you never thought to tell me this?'

'At the time, no. I seem to recall you wanted to get away. Besides, I'm telling you now.'

Ruben looked quickly across to Tom Yurling who had arrived to see what was going on.

'Never heard of any Virgil Prior,' he said, having heard the name Grace mentioned. 'I'd be surprised if he was any o' them things, though.'

'Is there anything else you can think of?' Ruben asked of Grace.

'No, I don't think so. I simply wanted to let you know I was wrong.'

Ruben nodded, holding her testing gaze.

Yurling muttered a goodnight. 'It's been a long day already an' only just got started,' he added and hurried out.

Ruben broke the awkward silence. 'I'm real obliged, Grace. But not knowing who this Prior is, I can't say more. But a friend of Datch's is also someone I'd be very wary of.'

Grace gave him a reserved smile. 'I thought you'd think that way. I won't be taking any money from Colvin Datch.'

'There'll be others.'

'I know.' Grace put her glass down. Then she got up and went to the door.

'That's decent liquor you haven't touched,' Ruben said, as she passed close to him.

'You have it. You know how to use a glass, don't you?'

'I'm a little out of practice, that's all. Goodnight, Grace. Thank you for dropping by.'

When she was gone, Ruben stood there looking out into the town. He had thought of escorting Grace back to the boarding house, but it wasn't that far to go. From where he stood, he could see her walk safely from door to door. He looked down at the glass of whiskey and laughed. The tension which had gripped him earlier had, for one reason or another, ebbed quietly away.

14

'Must've been one hell of a night.'

Having dozed off, Colvin Datch jumped at the sound of the voice. He swung about, his thumb impulsively drawing back the hammer of the jailhouse scattergun.

His son was lying on a bunk in the first cell. He lifted his head, twisted around to get a look at the newcomer. He saw a lean man about his own height, perhaps ten years older, wearing a slouch hat and holding a carbine at the side of his bleached duster.

'Virg,' Colvin Datch said with a mix of surprise and relief as he clambered to his feet. He laid the gun on the desk and extended his hand in greeting. 'I wasn't expectin' you this early. You've got things sorted?'

'A small bunch o' prime breedin' cows. An' they're bein' looked after better'n the good Lord's lambs.'

Datch's features creased into a grin as Bruno stepped from the cell.

'Virg, meet my boy . . . the sheriff of Bonachon, in all but name,' he introduced Bruno pretentiously. 'Bruno, meet Virgil Prior, your next deputy. He'll be seein' your body don't end up with more holes than it's got right now.'

Bruno gave an unenthusiastic nod. 'How do,' he said.

Colvin Datch's eyes darted knowingly between Prior and Bruno. 'All these goddamn years livin' from hand to mouth an' fouled with trouble,' he grumbled. 'But now I'm that close to gettin' what I want — guns to look out for me an' a town just waitin' to be taken. Hah, I've been loyal to that, if not much else. Yeah, I'll soon have this place so meek nobody will even *whisper* my name in vain.'

Virgil Prior grinned back at him. 'We'll take the pay, you do the thinkin', Cole. When's that goddamn saloon open?'

'Be an hour yet.' Datch went to the sheriff's desk, pulled out a canteen of Aguardiente and tossed it to Prior. 'This'll cut the dust ... keep you goin',' he said and watched the man take a wary swig. 'Now, you say you're holdin' that prize stock somewhere safe?'

'Yeah. We had a bit o' trouble with the former owner, but I took care o' him. The boys are keepin' a lid on things but they're rarin' to see somethin' o' the town.'

'They'll have to wait, Virg. When the buyer gets here, I'll take him straight out. Did you say when you'd be back?'

'Tonight.'

Datch thought for a moment. 'Fine, by then *you'll* be our deputy. Meantime, ride out an' tell the boys to sit tight. In a short while they can drink 'emselves to death for all I care,' he added.

Bruno Datch walked across the room and sluiced his face in the shallow basin. Prior watched him closely, sipping thoughtfully on the fiery liquor.

'Looks kind o' young, Cole. You sure he's as good as you say?' he said.

'Matched up to *you*, I wouldn't live long on the difference, I know that. But that won't be happenin', Virg. Workin' together, you two are my warrant to prosperity.'

'I just like to get peckin' orders sorted.'

'Bruno does what I tell *him* and you'll do what I tell *you*. Two days ago, the boy shot down Rites Noble.'

A cloud passed across Prior's face. 'Noble was good,' he said. 'Asleep at the time, was he?'

'No, Virg, he goddamn wasn't. It just never occurred to him he might be second best.'

Prior grunted something under his breath then drained the Aguardiente. He stood looking back out into the yard a moment before he spoke. 'What else has happened? You say you can get things done, like nominate an' elect peace officers. Well, that's a big claim for the time you've been in town.'

Datch grinned easy. 'Maybe I'm exaggeratin',' he admitted. 'Let me tell you a story.'

For the next five minutes, Datch related events of the last few days. 'So, now you know, an' here we are. You can see what I'm talkin' about, Virg,' he said. 'Have you got your own story right? Tell me.'

'I'm out o' Helendale where I deputized for the ol' stove-up, Monte Woods. But he's dead now, an' the town's under a Mojave sand blanket. I cut out, as anyone would. Only *half* that's true, but there's no reason to doubt *any* of it.'

'That's good, Virg. An' with me tellin' it, it's near to gospel. What are you doin' now?'

'Seein' to my horse an' waitin' for your barrel house to open.'

'OK. I'll meet you there. Remember, there's no link between us, an' only offer your services when I ask. No one's goin' to raise objections. Good deals are often struck in saloons. You need money?'

'Not yet. I'll make out.'

Prior gave Bruno another quick look and grinned. He pointed two fingers and clicked his tongue, like firing a kid's shooter. A few moments later, he was walking his horse from the back yard to the main street.

Bruno went to the front door and looked east towards the still rising sun. 'I'm not sure of him, Pa, except that I don't like him.'

'It's just his manner, son. Likin' don't have to figure. He'll tug your rope all right, but then he'll stay back. He can be pesky but he's good. Don't worry.'

Bruno wasn't satisfied, but he knew his father wouldn't tolerate more doubting. He stepped onto the board-walk; peering up and down the street, he wondered what was going to happen next.

★ ★ ★

'Mornin', Rube,' Tom Yurling said. 'I looked in earlier, saw your pallet hadn't been used.'

'No. Bit of a restless night, Tom, if you recall. I've been back to see Louis Barker. I suggested his tending to Marley Copper was heavily laudanum based for a day or two.'

'But that'll keep him there . . . at the doc's.'

'Yeah, if it's taken with some of Felix Shelter's house whiskey. It'll certainly keep him from being killed. We don't want him setting out for the Datches again. And go and see if Grace McSwane's got any ideas of the shape and size of her boarding school house. If I'm in the timber, I might as well cut some out. Tell her it'll be a donation.'

'For everythin'?'

'Not the building work. Someone else can pay for that. There's plenty needs what she's offering.'

Astride one of his chestnut saddlers, Ruben rode into the street where three of his yard men were waiting for him.

161

They discussed the tools and pack horse equipment, exchanged a few words about their route and procedure, before moving out.

Watching from the jailhouse, Colvin Datch saw the group turning sharp west at the end of town. 'It's the timin', son. It couldn't have been better if I'd *planned* it,' he said to Bruno. 'Let's get on. There's some good folk nearby keen to make you full sheriff.'

15

Along the boardwalk, Colvin Datch stopped at every store and business to invite anyone interested along to the Shelter Saloon. He reminded them of the previous night's trouble, convincing them that if the town was to be safer and better run, the meeting was to their advantage.

'Fortune's smilin', an' it favours the brave,' he told them. 'Maybe even a free drink.'

Ten minutes later he was standing at the bar with his first beer. 'Felix, you and me ain't exactly been buddies, an' I'm regrettin' our last one or two disagreements,' he said. 'So now I'm for buryin' the hatchet an' pickin' up the peace pipe. What do you say?'

Felix Shelter looked doubtful. 'I'd say you were in the wrong place at the wrong time,' he said, but accepted Datch's hand.

'Well, I'm proposin' the same to Ruben Ballard,' Datch continued. 'Hell, I know what a good man he is, an' good for Bonachon. I guess it's me who's been a little gritty over the years. But now my boy's in office, an' with Ballard an' his crew willin' to back up the law, I reckon we'll have a town as good as any in the territory. An' when the railroad decides to lay track up to Frisco, they'll add a spur line an' we'll all be floatin' on gold.'

Felix Shelter was having trouble thinking of somewhere other than Bonachon to compare it with. He had always been a one-town man, was curiously proud of it and he smiled easily in return.

'Goddamn it, Datch. If anyone had told me a week ago I'd hear you talk like that, I'd have stopped servin' 'em,' he said.

'Hah, I finally realized I've got responsibilities, Felix. I know a lot o' you folk are suspicious o' me bein' up in that jailhouse, but goddamn it, I'm only seein' my boy right, settin' him on the square. An' that's the time for me to leave. As soon as he's elected sheriff, an' got a trusty deputy.'

'Don't over-egg it,' Shelter replied. 'Bruno as sheriff?'

'Why not? That's what we're leadin' to. You know of a better man?'

Shelter, took a short, frustrated breath. 'Not in here right now, no. But somewhere out there, there'll be one.'

There was a discontented shuffle and murmur from the customers. They were obviously none too captivated by the full extent of what Datch had in mind.

'Bruno's not been a deputy much more'n overnight,' Shelter pressed. 'Goddamn it, he only just fits his suit.'

'Frankie Feathers was nineteen when he brought in the whole Legge family, wasn't he?' Datch countered.

'I was in Phoenix, Arizona when Kid Kease faced down Jim Buckley,' somebody down the counter added. 'He was only sixteen, an' made sheriff a year later. He did a fine job till some drunkard backshot him.'

Datch nodded eagerly. 'Wouldn't have happened if he'd had the trusty deputy behind him. But, like I was sayin', it's not age what matters, an' I reckon there's suitable candidates around us right here an' now. Hell, we've got the gun, all we need's the lingo that goes with it.' Datch stopped for a moment and eyed some new arrivals. Then he stepped away from the bar, holding up his hand for more attention.

'Just last night, my boy was in a place I'm sure none o' you men want to be in, let alone a peace officer. The jailhouse was attacked by men who came out o' the darkness to cut him down. If I hadn't been there to help, he'd be sleepin' deep this mornin' an' there'd be no law. So, despite what I said, I'm not goin' anywhere until I'm certain Bruno's given every chance.'

As Datch wiped beaded sweat from

his top lip, he saw Virgil Prior towards the other end of the saloon holding a glass of whiskey, but there was no sign of recognition. 'So it comes down to this,' he went on. 'In the shockin' face o' both Jefferson Kayte an' Silas Layborne gettin' killed, Bruno was elected deputy. He done himself proud, an' the way I see it, everythin's just about logically sorted with him set for sheriff.'

No one in the saloon moved or made a compliant sound. They weren't able to make up their minds and Datch cursed quietly as he stared around him.

'For chris'sake's, all you men got to do is vote for him an' a reliable deputy. Truth be told, I also see it as a vote to get *me* out o' that jailhouse. After last night, *that* won't be too goddamn soon,' he declared before turning to Felix Shelter.

'Felix, what you got to say? Seein' as how you don't always rely on a sawed-off piece to keep order, you'll know best that with Bruno, you get a man who can take out the dangerous trash like Rites Noble, or anyone else who steps out o' line. How'd you vote?'

Shelter looked uneasily about the room. For the first time he was conscious that Ruben Ballard wasn't there.

'I don't know as the time's right,' he said, unable to make up his mind on his own. 'There's one or two others who should be here if we're decidin' on who runs the town.'

'You're meanin' Ruben Ballard,' Datch stated.

'He'll be one of 'em, yeah. He's respected . . . prominent in the town.'

'Well, as it happens, I've seen him this mornin'. We chewed the ol' dog a bit, just like we're doin' here. He's out o' town right now, doin' some trade.'

'You told him your plans?' Shelter asked.

'o' course I did. That was the point. He's an interestin' man, Ruben Ballard. He conceded that him an' his men weren't enough to swing any vote against Bruno. But he also said he wouldn't speak out actively against him. As I say, he's an interestin' man, an' he's runnin' a cautious trail.'

'Cautious enough not to let you get too far off it,' Shelter cautioned.

'That's as maybe. But I'm standin' among men who've made lives an' got families they want to keep. For that, they need a young, tough sheriff. Preferably one who's backed by an older, experienced deputy. So, what about it, Felix? You takin' a middle trail, too . . . lettin' others decide for you? Or you votin' for Bruno . . . givin' him his chance?'

Felix Shelter licked his lips nervously. 'Not bein' spoiled for choice, I don't sees how I can vote against him. But he'll need a good man back of him.'

Virgil Prior began to shift down the room. He was the only man to move, causing all eyes to turn towards him. He drew a star badge from an inside pocket, flipped it lightly on the bar top in front of Shelter.

'Couldn't help but overhear your dilemma,' he said. 'Huh, I never figured I'd be usin' *this* again, even showin' it. It's been a sort of memento.'

Shelter picked up the tin star. 'Is it yours?' he asked.

'Yeah, it's mine. Strictly speakin', it's the property o' Helensdale. I just never returned it. Too late now, it's a ghost town. I've been on the drift for a while, but if you've been deputy to Monte Woods for five years, you lose interest in other ways of earnin' a crust.' Prior looked hard at Bruno Datch, the star sharp against the lapel of his dark suit. 'You kind o' remind me of ol' Monte. He never said much, either, an' I'm guessin' you're the one they're all so goosey about.'

'I'm Bruno Datch. Who are you?' Bruno replied.

'Virgil Prior,' the lean, weather-worn man said.

'Prior.' Colvin Datch considered as he moved closer. 'Name don't ring any bells. But I sure heard o' Monte Woods.

His name travelled well.'

'An' to lots o' places. I guess that's why I haven't been keen on workin' with anyone else. Perhaps things are changin' . . . someone's lucky day.'

'What're you tryin' to say?' Felix Shelter wanted to know.

'I'll stand deputy to this feller here, if you want it. I know the work, an' I can't ride on forever,' Prior suggested almost casually.

Colvin Datch took a quick look at the men who were becoming more interested in Virgil Prior. 'You got to give us more'n puffery to go on, Prior,' he said. 'You can't expect a town like Bonachon to put you in office without knowin' anythin' about you.'

'I don't. An' if it did, it wouldn't be the kind o' town I'd be pleased to work for,' Prior responded. 'What I'm saying is, I've been a deputy for five years and right now, whether it's happenstance or not, I'm probably the best you're likely to get. Like I heard someone say, out here you ain't exactly spoiled for choice. Without an affidavit, you want to see me do a Curly Bill spin? Maybe I can shoot a few folk?'

'Hah, no, no need for any o' that.' For a moment, Colvin Datch gave Prior a penetrating look. 'Maybe I'm not the best judge o' nature,' he said with a thin grin. 'But I reckon you're worth a risk. What about you, Bruno? He suit you as deputy?'

Bruno nodded compliantly. 'Why not? If he can see in the dark, all the better.'

Colvin Datch quickly moved his attention back to the other men. 'You've got Felix an' Bruno. Now let's hear from the rest o' you honest folk,' he said.

The men checked each other for a moment, but after Felix Shelter showed a hand, they gradually did the same.

Colvin Datch made a perfunctory count. 'No mistake there then,' he stated eagerly. 'Bruno for sheriff, an' if he's OK with Virgil Prior, I guess we all nailed it. Hah, it might take three or four months to get our Presidents elected, but in Bonachon we can do things a tad speedier.'

As Datch shook Bruno's hand, he took the beer from him. 'There's a better place for that, son,' he said and winked. 'Besides, it don't do for a sheriff to be under the influence while on duty. Certainly not a newly elected one. Now we'll get back to the jailhouse, an' I'll pack my sack.'

Datch and his son walked from the saloon. Virgil Prior stood finishing his drink.

'Which route was it they took for the jailhouse?' he asked of Felix Shelter.

'North. That's left, once you're outside o' here.' Shelter watched the new deputy pick up his saddle roll. It looked little more than a faded duster rolled tight around a Yellow Boy carbine. When Prior had gone, he leant over his counter at the thoughtful men about the bar.

'I wish Ruben had been here,' he said. 'We got ourselves a new sheriff, though I don't suppose his stockyard votes would have changed anythin'. Ol' Datch said there was a free drink in it, so I'll set him up a slate.'

Back at the jailhouse, Virgil Prior stood in the doorway watching Colvin Datch fold his gear. 'You are movin' out then?' he said.

'Of course. I want the peace keepin' team to get acquainted. The pair o' you's goin' to make out real good, so I'll go an' visit the boys. I want to know if Tedstone's bent on makin' any trouble.'

'He won't be.'

Datch stopped what he was doing. He stood up, turning to face Prior. 'Why'd you say that? What's happened to him?'

'He shot Flint. He left me no alternative.'

'I bet. Good job this place has a well out o' town bone yard. We don't have the goddamn room here,' Datch rasped dryly. 'What about his girls? There's two of 'em.'

Prior shook his head. 'Never saw any. Just him an' a rifle. He was out followin' our tracks, then he cut back to home ground. We were goin' to drive 'em straight through, not stop off for a goddamn gunfight.'

'That's the passin' of another goddamn bloodline,' Datch muttered and stomped around the jailhouse for a minute or so. Then he silently finished his packing, snatching it up from the bunk. 'Can't make it matter,' he said. 'I'll ride out an' see what's up. You sure he's dead?'

'He's got a fistful o' lead in him. Yeah, I'm sure.'

'For chris'sake's, Virg, you got to get this town to know you . . . to accept you. Let's have no more killin' until I get back. An' you, Bruno. No trouble. If Ballard returns, stay out of his way.'

'Who the hell's Ballard?' Prior asked.

'Owns the stockyard. Got money an' a mouth. He don't frighten easy, an' the town listens to him. Right now he's become sort o' quiet, but I don't trust him. He ain't the roll over sort.'

'I'll look out for him,' Prior said. 'Me an' young Bruno, that is.'

'You do that. I'm too long in this town.' With that, Colvin Datch nodded at Bruno, and went out to get a saddle across his rig horse.

16

George Stillman slowed the buckboard as he neared Tedstone's ranch house. He was curious about the total pall of silence. He knew that Jake Tedstone was always somewhere outside waiting when he brought the girls home.

Six turkey buzzards suddenly appeared on the far side of the barn's long, roof ridge, and instinct kicked in, telling him something was wrong. The same sense suggested that going in openly from the front wasn't the best approach and he decided to take a loop, using cover of the thick mesquite.

'Your pa didn't know we were comin' back today,' he said. 'We'll surprise him.' Stillman didn't turn to look at the girls as he spoke. He had an idea they too thought something was wrong.

'He's probably takin' an early siesta,' he offered uncertainly, turning the rig in a semi-circle beside the rear door. 'He'll be that pleased when he sees you.'

Moments later, Stillman cursed, breaking into a startled run when he saw the body at the bottom of the veranda steps. He went to his knees and brushed at the dust across Jake Tedstone's forehead, and looking down at the dark, blood-caked wounds, he cursed again.

Outraged and with his thoughts racing, he turned towards the house. He knew the girls were there by the front door watching him and he quickly lay Tedstone back down, stepping across to screen the body.

'Your pa's dead, girls. I'm sorry. Looks like some kind of heart attack,' he lied to their uncomprehending expressions.

'Why? He wasn't ill,' Annie, the youngest, said simply.

'That's what happens sometimes. It can creep up on you sudden. Both o' you go back the way you come in. Get back on board. I'll be with you in a minute. We're goin' straight back to my place.'

'Can I see him?' the eldest girl asked.

'Best you don't, Nancy. Remember him the way you saw him last. I'll take care o' things later.'

The girls nodded, looking miserably at each other. Although they couldn't understand the tragedy, they both knew what death meant.

★ ★ ★

It was late into the afternoon when Stillman saw Ruben Ballard walking from a timbered slope. Three other men were in a line behind, carrying single-bitted chip axes and log measurers.

Stillman ran his horse up close. 'Jake Tedstone's been killed,' he started, and drew rein. 'I found him out at the ranch. He was shot over an' over.'

'Where is he now?' Ruben asked.

'Town. I took the girls back to ours

179

then took him into the doc's. That's where I've come from.'

'Did his girls see him?'

'His body. Nothin' worse than that. I was bringin' 'em home.'

Ruben went to fetch his horse and speak to his men. 'Finish up here and go back to town. I've got something to do . . . might be gone for a while,' he told them.

It was an hour's ride to the Tedstone place. It didn't take long for Ruben to see where two horsemen had cut up the ground in the yard, where they'd swerved and reined in to shoot down Jake. He got back in the saddle and rode quickly to the home pasture where he saw the tracks of a small bunch heading direct south.

'They're going to San Bernardino,' he said. 'From there it'll be down to the Mexican border and one o' those hidalgo fellers . . . whatever they call them.'

'I reckon that's what Jake had in mind, too,' Stillman replied. 'They'll pay top dollar for the bloodline. Won't matter who bred or who's sellin' 'em.'

'Going for quality,' Ruben said, looking towards the distant mountain ranges. 'They freight east, all the way to Texas, and the whole process starts over. Jake would have seen something. Trouble was, there was three or four of them, and no one to help him out.'

'Someone's got to take care o' the girls,' Stillman said almost absent mindedly.

'I know someone who might be able to help,' Ruben answered eventually.

'Are you goin' after 'em, Ruben?'

'Oh yeah, I'm doing that all right. I've got a gut feeling.'

'I'll ride with you. I brought my ol' bird scarer. Don't do to get within thirty feet in any direction.' Stillman smiled grimly. Moments later, he nudged his sure-foot mount after Ruben.

They travelled for an hour before Ruben paused to check the ground more closely. 'Difficult being so few.

181

They've even got fancy feet that don't leave much of a stamp,' he said. 'But we can't push on any longer today, so why don't you take yourself home, George? You can pick me up in the morning.'

Stillman shook his head. 'Nah. I can't do that, Ruben. I can't face those girls. Not again today.'

Ruben understood the man's feelings. 'That's OK. We can make cold harbour and start early.'

Within ten minutes, they were settled down, each of them with his own thoughts, his immediate plans for the day ahead.

For Ruben, Jake Tedstone was a man who'd done little or no harm. He had simply wanted progress, to improve the qualities of everything within his reach, and that included his select herd of Herefords as well as Annie and Nancy.

For the first time, Ruben felt the cold knot of avenging anger tighten inside him.

★   ★   ★

Colvin Datch wasted no time in driving to Jake Tedstone's ranch. For an hour, and with increasing alarm, he searched the house, outbuildings and nearby land. No body meant that someone else must have been there, discovered what happened, how Tedstone had died.

Anxious, Datch headed south towards the first stand of Joshua trees where he had ordered the stolen Herefords to be taken. He knew the route, and a low, late sun slanted the country when he picked up the tracks of the herd.

'Hold up there, mister,' the voice called out. 'Give us a name we know.'

Datch reined in, turned and looked at the rifle barrel that was pointed at him. 'It's me, goddamn it. The man who's payin' you,' he rasped back.

'Hell, boss!' Polk Meade exclaimed and lowered his rifle. 'You're nothin' like Virg. We were expecting him.'

'He's got other stuff on his mind,' Datch told him, immediately heeling his horse up a rocky dune where he could see the small herd.

'Beautiful beasts. Tedstone knew what he was doin',' he said. 'I'm gettin' fifty dollars a head from those chili señors, an' no questions asked. Hah, not that I'd understand if there was.'

'Yeah. That's what I like to hear. Just make sure they pay in greenbacks.' Meade laughed and moved alongside Datch. 'I don't suppose you got any liqueur on board?' he asked.

'There's no booze till you hit town. Don't you ever think of anythin' else?'

'Yeah. But last time I got a slap for it. So what you got in Bonachon?'

'With my boy as sheriff, an' Virgil as deputy, the lot . . . or will have. We wait till the end o' the week, an' after gettin' rid o' these cows, we'll cut back. What happened with Jake Tedstone?'

'*He* stopped Chavez, an' Virg stopped *him*. *We* were standin' off with the herd.'

'An' you left him there . . . Tedstone?'

'Hell, yeah. I guess Virg figured coyotes an' buzzards would do their bit.'

'Stupid,' Datch snarled. 'You reckon they swallow belts an' boot leather?'

'We're not paid to reckon on anythin', boss. Just to bring the dumb critters out here.'

'Tedstone's got two girls.' Datch continued his thinking. 'Where the hell were they? They'll be back, an' someone's already taken care o' Tedstone.'

Datch rode on until he reached the puncheoned line shack that was shared between Stillman and Tedstone. The fruity interior heat overwhelmed him when he peeled aside the hide-flapped door. He backed off and cursed, looked down at the dry, broken mesquite at his feet.

'I hope you two haven't been lightin' any goddamn fires,' he rasped angrily.

'We got to eat,' Meade answered back. 'Hell, all we do's mollycoddle these hairy critters. We daren't leave 'em alone for more'n a few minutes. Lettin' 'em sashay wherever they want, then watchin' for anythin' that might spook 'em.'

'They're line bred stock, Meade. Somethin' that few of us know little about. So, from now on, there'll be no risks with fires. I'm not seein' my plans loused up by a plate o' hot beans. An' we got some talkin' to do about what happens before an' after you an' Beggs get to town . . . my town.'

Meade grunted out an OK, and sauntered off. He was thinking that if Datch had ideas on actually taking over a town, he just might have a big worm in his brain.

'There'll be grub in the cabin if you're tough enough to go in an' get it. Or we can get our heads down for a few hours,' Datch muttered, hardly aware that no one was listening.

17

Ruben Ballard and George Stillman threaded their way through the tight stands of greasewood, emerging to look upon a vast, powdery scrape of desert.

'Stretches to the California Gulf,' Ruben said.

Stillman studied him with tired concentration. 'Yeah, this is the way they've come. There's a way around, further to the east, but it's goin' to take another week.'

'Beyond the next ridge the country gets poorer . . . much poorer. There's not much cover and less to drink. But along the Santa Rosa is the best, maybe quickest route to Mexico,' Ruben said. 'If there was someone on my tail, it's the way I'd go.'

Stillman shook his head. 'No, you wouldn't. The heat off the sand would fry your brain before you got halfway.'

'It's quickest for a payout.'

'It's more'n a hundred miles, Ruben. They'll all die.'

'So where the hell else can they go?'

'Bonachon. We're out *here*, they'll be in *there*. There's no reason for anyone to suspect, an' Jake won't be sayin'. It makes some sort o' sense.'

'Not much. But OK. We'll ride east, see what we can pick up.'

Two hours later, they stepped from the bed of a dry wash. Ruben felt the lightest of breezes across his face, a familiar scent in the air.

'It sure ain't any sweet smellin' mariposa,' Stillman remarked.

'It's got to be Tedstone's herd, George. You were right, and they're just ahead of us.'

A mile on, standing in the shade of more greasewood, the two men stared at the quietly milling Herefords.

'How many guns?' Ruben asked.

'Three. One of 'em near the cabin. How about inside?'

'I doubt it in this heat. Let's settle for

those we can see. Best way's to circle from behind, I guess. We've got surprise riding with us, so we'll ride close. Are you sure you want in on this, George?'

Stillman lifted the barrel of his old scattergun. 'I saw what they did to Jake. It'll be for his kids,' he said seriously.

'I understand,' Ruben agreed. 'But I don't want to be the one to take bad news back to *your* family.'

Stillman shook his head, gave a thin smile. 'I know. But I'm not even plannin' to get myself wounded by those sons o' bitches. Besides, I've never heard of any cow thief standin' ground under a rancher's attack.'

'So, what are we waiting for?' Ruben said, turning his horse back into the yucca. He was going for a longer, circling approach on the cattle and the three men holding them.

It was mid-morning now and the sun was blazing down. Men and cattle alike becoming hazy, shifting shapes across the western Mojave.

Ruben exchanged a conspiratorial

look with Stillman. 'Don't let me get too far ahead,' he said, before putting his heels to his horse. He charged from cover of the greasewood, heading directly for the riders who were nudging the Herefords towards the line shack.

He was within thirty yards of Beggs, when the man looked up and saw him. Beggs immediately dashed for his Colt, but Ruben was considering the distance and curbed his response.

When they were fifty or sixty feet apart, Beggs fired off his first shot. But Ruben was approaching with the sun above and behind him. Beggs's shot was panicky and went wide, his second closer but still off target. The man swore and turned away, deciding to make a fearful run for it.

Ruben had pulled his horse to a halt. He raised his Colt, took steady aim and calmly fired twice.

Beggs's head dropped and his arms fell to his sides a moment after taking both Ruben's bullets. With no control, the horse skittered in alarm and Ruben saw the rider collapse forward, then topple sideways from the saddle.

Polk Meade was riding back to give support, but when he saw Beggs fall, he dragged his horse about in a tight circle.

When Meade turned, George Stillman had a standing target for a moment. He fired off his scattergun, and Meade jerked, then hunched down. Losing the reins, Meade stretched out a hand, his fingers desperately grasping for his mount's dark mane.

But now Ruben was running at him. As he regained control of his horse, and attempted to lift his Colt, another of Ruben's paired bullets ripped across his shoulder and low into his neck.

A harsh, guttural sound erupted from Meade. He tried once more to drag up his Colt, but was dead before he fell to the ground.

Spooked by the shooting, the small herd broke into a frightened run. Ruben looked for Stillman, waving for him to follow into the thin roil of dust.

They were heading for the line shack. Ruben kept low, trying to estimate when to break away, confront the last of the three men up close.

Breathing fast and shallow, Ruben chose his moment. He ran his horse straight for the doorway where a man was kneeling with a rifle tight to his shoulder. He felt a hammer blow to the right side of his ribs, and he gasped, reined in hard and dropped to the ground. He held his Colt steady in both hands and took aim. Then his fingers froze as shock registered, the return of gut wrenching anger when recognition broke through.

'Datch. You, you murdering scum,' he rasped.

Colvin Datch twisted back against the hide door. He stood his ground, his jaw working savagely. 'Goddamn, Ballard,' he snarled. 'Why couldn't you stay out of it?'

Ruben realized the target he'd become, but suddenly he was a tad beyond fully caring. In fact, a number of things which had worried him for days suddenly got clearer; like Colvin Datch pushing to get his son established in office. It was part of a bigger picture, a megalomaniac's fantasy. The killing of Jake Tedstone was a big mistake, a serious trip on the way up.

As he walked resolutely into the line of fire, another bullet chewed the outside of his upper leg, and it stopped him. But it wasn't enough to put him down, and cursing freely, he used his Colt.

The .44 bullet hammered high into Datch's chest, sending him up against the crumbling doorframe. The next shot to strike him was almost in the same spot. He dropped the rifle and turned, grasping at the hide-flap door as he fell into the stinking darkness of the line shack.

Grimacing, Ruben limped forward. He used the barrel of his Colt to hold the heavy flap aside.

Colvin Datch, fallen with his face against the dirt floor, wasn't much aware of the wedge of light that suddenly fell across him.

'It wasn't your business,' he spat painfully. He started to repeat himself, but only a shallow breath came before he died.

'True. But it wasn't yours, either,' Ruben muttered in return. He fired down at Datch once again, but the hammer fell on a spent chamber. 'Well, what do you know,' he added with bitter irony.

Stepping around Datch, Ruben forced himself to take a quick look inside the line shack. When Stillman pulled up, he showed him what he had in his hand.

'I put in my two cents' worth,' the rancher confirmed anxiously. 'Where'd you get that from?'

'On the floor beside Datch's body. Somebody must have dropped it.'

'A tobacco tin?'

'Yeah, silver. Made in Mexico, I

reckon. It's got the initial P stamped on the lid.'

'You know who it belongs to?'

'I think so. Grace McSwane mentioned someone who was a friend . . . a business associate of Datch. He was of timely importance, apparently. She said his name, and I'm sure it began with a P.'

Stillman nodded. 'If he's an important feller, we need to return it. Do you reckon he's in Bonachon?'

'Yeah, I do. Let's get Datch back into the saddle.'

After folding Datch across the rig horse, Ruben spoke earnestly to Stillman. 'Sorry, George, you won't be coming with me,' he said. 'You can leave those other two for the buzzards, or throw them in here. Burn it down, for all I care. But get yourself back home.'

'I'll definitely do the last bit. Thanks, Ruben, an' good luck.'

18

On the way back to town, Ruben stopped to meet up with his men and tell them what had happened. 'We've dealt with half of them, and that still leaves Bonachon in dangerous shape,' he said.

The two stockyard men who had been estimating and marking timber listened with concern.

'Right now, it makes measurin' trees a bit pointless,' one of them said. 'We'll ride back with you, if that's OK.'

It was late afternoon when the three men rode into town, behind long sundown shadows that pointed along the main street.

At the yard, Ruben left Colvin Datch's body in one of the open-sided barns. He asked the men to throw straw around him. 'It's how to store beef when there's nothing else,' he said.

He checked and reloaded his Colt at his office, then went directly to the Shelter Saloon. Reading the situation as volatile, Tom Yurling and the two hands Ruben had returned to town with, followed on closely.

Watching from the front window of the boarding house, Grace McSwane uttered a few unschoolma'am-like words. She had never seen anything like the deep rage Ruben Ballard was obviously carrying inside him. After the long hours of rumour and guesswork, she hurried out to the street, looking with anticipation at other people gathering along the boardwalk.

'I sure wouldn't want to be in the bunch that he's lookin' for. It's been a year or two since I seen him like that,' one man said.

'Do you know what's happened . . . what's going on?' Grace asked him.

'No, but *he* sure does, ma'am. Whatever it is, it involves young Datch, an' that new feller. Right now I'd rather be ten miles away, an' I ain't done nothin'.'

Grace realized with a sudden shock that *she* didn't think that. Ruben Ballard mattered to her. When she reached the saloon, she declined the offer to step inside when a man held the door open for her. The place was busy and voices were being raised, but there was no doubt Ruben was asking the whereabouts of Virgil Prior and Bruno Datch.

'So, where are they now, goddamn it? You're the ones here in town,' she heard him ask impatiently.

'Last I heard they were up at the jailhouse. I don't see they're goin' to be anywhere else,' Felix Shelter replied.

Moments later, the men in the saloon stood aside and Grace was suddenly face to face with Ruben. His expression was now more callous, and he looked at her in what looked like utter detachment.

'Ruben, what is it? Where are you going? Please tell me.' The anxiety cut

198

the normal composure of her voice, but it made Ruben stop in mid stride. He looked at her as he would a stranger, but then he blinked, brought his mind back.

'Sorry,' he said. 'It's Colvin Datch. He had Jake Tedstone killed and took his cattle, his prize herd. I'm guessing that would have been the source of your building money. He put his boy in office, his pet gun, to make sure there's no trouble. And now it's about a man named Virgil Prior who's here to back up whatever else he's got in mind. That's what it is, Grace, and I've got to go and sort it out.' With that, Ruben tipped his hat and moved off down the boardwalk.

Grace was astonished that no one appeared to be going with him. Even Tom Yurling seemed reluctant, following on at a distance.

'He's going alone?' she shouted angrily. 'Is this the town and its people he's looking out for? None of you are going to help him?'

Felix Shelter was soon alongside her. 'It don't do to go with Ruben Ballard at times like this, Miss McSwane,' he said. 'Believe me, he don't think any less of us for stayin' out of it. Right now it looks mighty convenient to be thinkin' like that, but we all know he can't be stopped an' he can't be helped.'

The colour drained from Grace's face, and now she felt sick, unsteady on her feet. 'I don't think 'convenient' is quite the right word, Mr Shelter,' she muttered dejectedly.

★   ★   ★

Virgil Prior drew back from the jailhouse window. 'I don't like the look or the feel o' this,' he said. 'It's not shapin' up the way I thought.'

Sitting at the sheriff's desk, Bruno Datch had been quietly toying with various accoutrements of office for over an hour. Prior knew he was worrying about his father's hasty departure from town, tense because he was undertaking duties he had no real aptitude for.

'What is it you don't like the look of?' Bruno asked.

'The feller who rode in. There was some other riders with him, an' from the fuss made, you'd think he was some kind o' senator. Yeah, him by the stockyard,' Prior added as Bruno stepped up beside him.

'That's Ruben Ballard, an' he owns it.' Bruno's expression soured. 'Pa said he was tradin' out o' town. I didn't think he'd be back for a few days.'

'Well, clearly he is. I think I'll take a walk over there an' take a look at him . . . see what's goin' on.'

Bruno looked directly at Prior. 'No. Pa said to keep away if he came back. You were there.'

'You got the flutters over a cow an' mule man?'

Bruno shook his head. 'Over my pa. So we'll just do like he said. If he comes back an' says to go see what's happened, I will.'

Prior cursed under his breath. He'd

waited weeks for Colvin Datch to contact him, to earn some cash and get to town, throw his weight around and enjoy the benefits of authority. He didn't think bunking in the jailhouse with a young pretender was bringing that work much closer.

'So what do we do meantime?' he snapped.

'You do whatever you want, Prior. I've got some stuff to think about.' Doggedly, Bruno sat back down.

'To think about?' Prior exclaimed.

'Yeah. I was thinkin' there was some sense in all o' this, but I can't figure it. What Pa really wants for this town . . . for me. You comin' along, an' Jake Tedstone gettin' shot for his cattle.'

Prior looked amazed. 'There must be some goose in you, Bruno. You really can't figure it?'

Bruno shook his head slowly. 'No. Tell me.'

Prior had another look out the window, then crossed the room to sit corner-wise on the edge of the desk.

For a few seconds he studied Bruno carefully. 'Well, Bruno, you're either a real lunkhead, or your pa's a lot smarter than most everyone thinks. I'm guessin' we're somewhere in between. You've gone along with what he's told you, while he's pullin' off the stunt of his life.'

'Sounds real excitin'. What's it mean?'

'Your pa, Bruno. He reckons that in a year — with you cock o' the walk, an' me workin' close — he can tuck half the territory under his wing. Squeeze it dry then take control of its business.'

'And what about the killings?'

'To start with he had to remove Jefferson Kayte. But Rites Noble stepped in an' did it for him. Sure, he hadn't got it planned that way, but he soon saw somethin' to his advantage.'

'What was that?'

'A smarter, better lookin' way of doin' things, like gettin' you elected as deputy. Then there was Silas Layborne.'

'Layborne? Pa killed him?' Bruno's

forehead knotted in consternation.

'Yeah. Another scrupulous lawman, what he said . . . what he didn't want. I heard he finagled some poor kid into standin' trial for it.'

'How'd he benefit from that?'

'It gave you both a station. The jailbreak attempt helped him better than if he'd planned it himself. It left you runnin' solo with no opposition. He's gettin' money from Tedstone's prime beef to buy himself into town society. Hah, it's better'n one o' them half-dime novels.'

'What's he doin' now?'

'Right now? He's seein' his cattle . . . remindin' Polk an' Beggs what happens next. You an' me run down anybody who tries to stop us squarin' the circle.'

Bruno's features were tight with concern and sweat was beading lightly across his face.

'That's lies. Pa made plans for me to get on, an' he's never robbed or killed anyone.'

Prior shook his head. 'Where *has* he had you stashed away all this time?' he mocked.

'How come he told *you* all this?'

'Loyalty. He knew if he wanted mine, he had to let me in on a secret. It works most times. With you, I guess it was a question of what you don't know can't hurt you . . . or him.'

Prior saw the anger in Bruno Datch's eyes, the hurt of being used. He knew he'd brought him into the open, and at that moment grew wary. There wasn't much argument left in Bruno, only pent-up danger.

'OK, have it your way,' he said in a less antagonistic tone. 'But when he comes back, we'll talk. I reckon there's some misunderstandin' with the way things are, you not knowin' what the hell's goin' on. As I said, I don't like the look or feel of it.'

Bruno stared at Prior. His loathing for the man was growing with every word they exchanged.

Prior, feeling he was marginally

ahead of a threatening situation, went back to the window. 'It looked to me like there was a stiff rode in with 'em. But they must've offloaded him, an' now they're headed for the saloon,' he said. 'Tell me about Ballard.'

'He's got friends. An' not just them he's bought or owe him. Folks seem to go with what he says.'

Prior glanced quickly at Bruno, saw his features become more thoughtful, maybe even respectful. 'In that case, we'd better both go an' see what he's up to. He wasn't just goin' in to cut the dust,' he stated.

'No.' Bruno banged the bottoms of his fists down on the desk. 'Pa wanted him left alone. We're the lawmen in this town, an' if there's trouble, they'll come to us with it.'

Prior answered after a moment or two. 'Yeah. An' I think your Ruben Ballard's decided to do just that, Sheriff. Which means he's either very stupid, very brave or very good,' he said, slow and thoughtful.

★   ★   ★

Stepping down from the boardwalk, backing halfway across the narrow main street, thirty feet from the jailhouse door, Ruben waited a moment before calling out. 'Hey, you two. You know I'm here. There's one or two things we need to talk about.'

From outside the Shelter Saloon, Grace McSwane could hardly breathe with the tension. Silence filled the street. She saw Virgil Prior walk out first; the stranger who'd arrived in town to get himself elected deputy sheriff. Now she knew that Ruben Ballard's suspicions were right, and the coolness of first dark suddenly chilled.

'I saw you ride in with someone slung across a saddle. Guessed you'd be payin' us a visit. Who was it?' Prior directed back at Ruben.

'It's Colvin Datch. I thought Bruno should know.'

Bruno was already stepping from his office to the boardwalk. 'Pa?' he asked disbelievingly from beside Prior.

'Yeah. Your pa, Bruno. He *was* riding with Jake Tedstone's cattle. *Now* he's over at the yard. It was him behind the killing. He's to blame for all the bad stuff that's happened in Bonachon the last few days.'

'What the hell are you talkin' about?' Bruno yelled.

'For hell's sake, you're wearing a badge because he wanted to use you, too. Your deputy's a killer, and he helped run off the bunch of Herefords. That's why I'm here now. That, and to return a souvenir he left behind.'

Virgil Prior snorted loudly. He looked along the street, saw the slowly advancing, confrontational crowd.

'Your friends are dead, Prior. They tried hard not to be,' Ruben pushed. 'So you don't get backed up on this. Not even by the town sheriff.'

Prior cursed, reached quickly and angrily for his Colt.

But Ruben knew what he was doing. His provoking words were considered and he'd already made a move fraction-ally before Prior. It made him that much the quicker of the two.

Prior pulled his gun, but that was all he managed. He caught two bullets from Ruben's Colt even before he knew he was beat. He spat venomously as his legs buckled. 'My chaw box,' he garbled. 'Wondered where it was.'

Bruno Datch hadn't made a move. Briefly shocked with what Ruben had confronted him with, his mind was hopping. Then, as Prior crumpled lifeless, in front of him, rage took over.

'You killed my pa, Ballard,' he accused, taking a step back.

'That's a fair assumption, Bruno,' Ruben replied coolly. 'Nonetheless, I've no fight with you. I think your pa had you fooled like the rest of us. Apart from me an' Jeff Kayte, that is. I reckon I've settled what I came here to do.'

'Not yet,' Bruno objected. 'You're not walkin' away. Not for what you did.'

Ruben knew it wasn't an idle threat.

But he didn't want to kill Bruno, or try. He'd prefer to send him away with a lot to think about; send him packing with a shovel to bury his pa someplace.

'I can sort of understand you, Bruno,' he said. 'But the way you are right now, you'll be making me stop you. You're in the wrong and it's going to make a difference. For you . . . not a good one.'

'Damn you,' Bruno seethed intolerantly and went for his gun.

Ruben pulled his Colt for a second time in less than a minute. But now, it was two .44 bullets that slammed into Bruno Datch's chest.

Bruno coughed, gave a strange pleading look that crumpled his features. Then he staggered back across the doorway as if wanting refuge in the jailhouse. Either that or to hide the shame of dying.

Ruben pushed his Colt hard back in his holster. He thought Bruno had made a fast enough draw, but he'd gone no further. He'd hardly raised his arm to fire, as though he'd no intention of striking back.

The only certainty was both Datches were now dead. There was nothing Ruben could do and he cursed and turned away. He looked along the street, wondered if there might be someone who had seen the fight, and shared the same misgivings about Bruno Datch's participation. But there was no one except Grace McSwane who appeared to be ahead of the crowd.

Ruben gave a look which he hoped looked like he was pleased to see her, then he headed straight for his stock-yard.

He got back at the same time as Grace. Oblivious to what lookers-on might make of it, she'd hurried to catch up, purposefully twisting her way inside the office just ahead of him.

'Yeah. Getting to the Wild Turkey before me. Just imagine how *I* feel,' he muttered tiredly.

While Grace poured one large measure into a glass and another into a tin mug, Ruben took off his hat and gunbelt and tossed them carelessly onto his desk.

'It looks like you aim to stay and drink it this time,' he added.

In the main street, some people were now standing at the door of the jailhouse, looking in at the body of Bruno Datch. They were shaken, unable to believe that for a handful of days the town had been put on the squeeze by Colvin Datch; could only speculate on why the man had carried so much anger and resentment for so many years.

'I've been around long enough to know that sadly, most bad boys make bad men,' Billy Vane said.

'Yeah, but only *most*, Billy. We'll never know if Bruno was the exception,' Felix Shelter replied. 'But I know his pa still owes me for a round o' drinks.'

'We need to get these bodies away from here,' someone else said. 'At least it'll look like we're back to normal.'

★ ★ ★

'I'm sort of obliged to stay here,' Ruben was telling Grace. 'At least until someone finds a couple of redoubtable souls to man the law office.'

'And then what?' she asked.

'For some time I've been meaning to take a trip. Headed west, the ocean's not much more than a hundred miles, and the air won't smell of cow and cordite.'

'The town's suddenly got used to you sorting things out.'

Ruben shrugged. 'I'll give them six months. Then, they'll have to get by with someone else. I'll be doing them a big favour.'

'Am I included in that?'

'No, Grace. I'd like for you to come with me. If *you'd* like, of course. I guess that depends on you and your boarding school.'

'Yes. I owe them it. Everyone who's supported me. But I'm not sure how to continue. The endowment was real enough, even if what was behind it wasn't. So, where do I go from here?'

'You need an alternative proposal,' Ruben suggested. 'I reckoned on paying for the timber, but why stop there? It's already been pointed out to me I've made a few dollars over the last few years. This way I'll see something in return . . . something worthwhile. How long do you reckon it'll take to be up and running?'

'Six months to make sure I had it right.'

'There you go.' Ruben smiled and raised his drink.

'That's it, then. But can a schoolteacher take on such an enterprise without a chaperone?'

'I hear there's a Mission in Santa Barbara that's got its own priest. We can stop off and ask him if there's a way round it.'

We do hope that you have enjoyed reading this large print book.

Did you know that all of our titles are available for purchase?

We publish a wide range of high quality large print books including:
**Romances, Mysteries, Classics
General Fiction
Non Fiction and Westerns**

Special interest titles available in large print are:
**The Little Oxford Dictionary
Music Book, Song Book
Hymn Book, Service Book**

Also available from us courtesy of Oxford University Press:
**Young Readers' Dictionary
(large print edition)
Young Readers' Thesaurus
(large print edition)**

For further information or a free brochure, please contact us at:
**Ulverscroft Large Print Books Ltd.,
The Green, Bradgate Road, Anstey,
Leicester, LE7 7FU, England.
Tel:** (00 44) 0116 236 4325
Fax: (00 44) 0116 234 0205

Other titles in the
Linford Western Library:

NOLAN'S LAW

Lee Lejeune

After his mother and father die, and the girl he hopes to marry turns him down, Jude James decides to abandon his rented homestead and ride for the West along with Josh, a young exslave seeking sanctuary. Eventually they fall in with a gang led by Brod Nolan, who claims to rob the rich to feed the poor. But there is more to this than meets the eye — and the two friends find themselves embroiled in a series of bloodcurdling encounters in which they must kill or be killed . . .

PIRATES OF THE DESERT

C. J. Sommers

The locals call the sand dunes of the Arizona Territory southland a white ocean. One man, Barney Shivers, carries the comparison a little further when he orders his men to attack any freight shipping that he does not control, and steal the goods on board. A little old lady, Lolly Amos, contracts her nephew, Captain Parthenon Downs of the Arizona rangers, to fight back. Downs eagerly takes on the challenge — but little does he realize that his decision will draw him into a war against two bands of pirates . . .

THE VIGILANCE MAN

Fenton Sadler

For twelve-year-old Brent Cutler, seeing his father lynched was the most powerful influence on his young life, giving him an abiding and lifelong hatred of injustice in any form. As an adult, he returns to the town where he grew up, as a representative of the District Attorney's office — and finds himself going head to head with the man responsible for the death of his father a decade earlier. There will be hard words and tough actions before Cutler can finally lay the demons of his childhood to rest.